All's Fair in Love, War, and High School

Also by Janette Rallison

PLAYING THE FIELD

Janette Rallison

WALKER & COMPANY
NEW YORK

All the characters and events portrayed
in this work are fictitious.

First published in the United States of America in 2003
by Walker Publishing Company, Inc.

Published simultaneously in Canada by
Fitzhenry and Whiteside, Markham, Ontario L3R 4T8

For information about permission to reproduce
selections from this book, write to Permissions,
Walker & Company, 435 Hudson Street,
New York, New York 10014

Library of Congress Cataloging-in-Publication Data
Rallison, Janette, 1966–
All's fair in love, war, and high school / Janette Rallison.—
[1st American ed.]
p. cm.
Summary: When head cheerleader Samantha Taylor does poorly on
the SAT exam, she determines that her only hope for college
admission is to win the election for student body president, but her
razor wit and acid tongue make her better suited to dishing out
insults than winning votes.
ISBN 0-8027-8874-2
[1. High schools—Fiction. 2. Schools—Fiction.
3. Self-perception—Fiction. 4. Elections—Fiction.] I. Title.
PZ7.R13455A1 2003
[Fic]—dc21
2003042299

Book design by Jennifer Ann Daddio

Visit Walker & Company's Web site at www.walkeryoungreaders.com

Printed in the United States of America

2 4 6 8 10 9 7 5 3

To Devon,

who was the greatest prom date.

To Shawn,

who I'm sure knows why.

To Tim,

whose relentless editing made all the difference.

To the Rallison clan.

And to Katerina Chernikova,

who will always be our Katya.

Special note to all my friends from Pullman:

The characters in this story are purely fictional, but if you think I may have written you into the book, by all means buy three or four copies because hey, how cool.

All's Fair in Love, War, and High School

The problem with getting bad news is you hardly ever get to go home and cry, or sulk, or rip things up, like you'd like to. Usually you have to be someplace that requires you to smile and make pleasant conversation. That's exactly what happened after I got my SAT scores.

I should have waited until after work to open up the envelope, but I'm not one of those patient types of people—you know, the kind who never even sneak a peek at their presents before Christmas. I had to know my score the moment I took the letter from the mailbox. I ripped open the envelope and scanned to the score results. I got a 470 on the language section and a 340 on the math. My score was 810 out of a possible 1600. I may have bombed the math portion of the test, but even I could figure out my score wasn't high enough to be admitted to a good university.

I leaned against the mailbox and reread the letter more carefully this time, hoping there had been some mistake. Perhaps a typo. Perhaps the SAT people sent somebody else's results in my envelope. But it was my name, Samantha Taylor, on the letter.

I shoved the envelope into my purse and walked over to my car. I had ten minutes to get to my job, and apparently a really long time to decide what to do with my life besides going to college.

While I drove I told myself everything would work out all right. I was only a junior in high school and could take the SATs again next year. Next year I'd do better. Much better.

Only I'm a terrible liar, and even while I told myself all of this, I kept hearing a little voice in the back of my head that said, *Like what? You're suddenly going to get smart in the next year? You're going to give up your social life and study every free minute?*

I parked my car and walked into The Bookie, Pullman's only bookstore, then trudged upstairs to the general fiction section.

Logan Hansen was standing behind the book cart, but he looked up at me when I came over.

"You're late."

"So fire me." I went to the closet where Mr. Donaldson kept our vests and slipped mine on.

Logan handed me a stack of books. "I wouldn't fire you if I could. It's nice to have you around because next to you I look like a really hardworking employee."

I smiled back at him. "Next to me you also look ignorant and poorly dressed, but I try not to hold it against you." Without waiting for his reply, I turned and went to put my books away. Usually I didn't mind sparring back and forth with Logan. Most of the time I was the one who started it. But today I just wanted to avoid him. I felt too emotional, and the last thing I needed was to break down and make a fool of myself in front of him.

Logan and I had been at odds with each other since the eighth grade, when I broke up with him. It wasn't that we were ever a serious couple. "Going out" consisted mostly of passing notes, hanging out in the halls, talking on the phone, that sort of thing.

We "went out" for a couple of months, and then the big realization hit me. Logan was not *the one*. In fact, if I'd had a list of my favorite guys, Logan would have been way down in the triple digits. My problem with guys is this: I always start out thinking that if a guy is cute, he'll be perfect in every other way. Then after a couple of months of getting to know him, I realize he isn't anywhere close to what I want in a boyfriend. I don't remember what turned me off about Logan. He exhibits so many irritating behaviors now, it's hard to recall which one it was that bothered me back then. And besides, I've gone out with a lot of guys. Their fatal flaws have all run together in my mind.

My last boyfriend swore too much. The first time my seven-year-old brother repeated one of his commentaries at the dinner table, I knew he had to go. The boyfriend before that talked endlessly about the guys on the football team. I mean, really. What girl wants to hear about the team's ongoing battle with athlete's foot?

I don't know why it's so hard for me to find just one ideal guy. I've probably read a hundred romances, and every single one of them has my ideal man in it. So they must be out there somewhere: all those tall, handsome, brooding men who exude high doses of testosterone yet, at the same time, can take a woman in their arms and murmur poetry into her ear.

None of the guys I meet are capable of murmuring anything that doesn't involve food.

Logan walked by me and said, "We've got another book

cart to unload in the back room, so get a move on," then disappeared into the maze of bookshelves.

Logan, for example, could never have qualified as a romantic hero. True, he wasn't bad-looking. He had thick dark hair and a smooth olive complexion that always made him look tanned, but not one of the romantic heroes I've ever read about has dirt underneath his fingernails. Logan loves to work on cars. He looks like he dips his hands in oil before he comes to work.

Besides, he took it very hard when I broke up with him in junior high. He told all of his friends I was a jerk and a snob, and ever since then he's taken it as his personal mission to prove how worthless I am. A romantic hero would never do that. If a romantic hero was ever hurt by a girl, he'd never stoop to sullying her name. He'd just brood about it and be all the more attractive.

While I was shelving the next batch of books Logan came up and leaned against the end shelf.

"So," he said slowly, "how are you today?"

I barely looked over at him. "Fine. What do you want?"

He put his hand to his chest, pretending to be hurt. "I'm just making polite conversation. Don't you do that anymore?"

"If you're asking me to take your shift on Friday night, I'm not interested."

"Oh? You must have a hot date. Who's the lucky guy?"

He said the word "lucky" really sarcastically, so I glared at him. "Brad Willis."

"Brad Willis, huh? A guy with both the build and the intelligence of a semi truck. A perfect match for you."

I shoved my copies of Dr. Spock onto the shelf with a *thunk*. "Yeah, well, I'd tell you who your perfect match is, but I don't know anyone with the personality of a broken-down bicycle."

I walked back to the cart, and Logan followed me. "Are you and Brad serious?"

"We've been going out for a month and a half."

"So you're about through with him then?"

I forced a smile on my lips. "No, but I'm through with you. Go away."

"I didn't mean to be rude," he said with a perfectly straight face. "I was just asking because I know someone who wants to go out with you."

"Oh? Who?"

Logan hesitated for a moment, as though he wasn't sure he should come right out and tell me, then said, "Now, correct me if I'm wrong, but you aren't into guys who are big in the brains department, right?"

"I went out with you, didn't I?" I meant it as an insult. I meant I was agreeing with him and using him as an example of the stupidity of my boyfriends.

"Yeah," he said, "but *for the most part* the guys you date aren't heavy on the *I* part of IQ, right?"

There's nothing more frustrating than insulting someone who doesn't get it. "Just tell me who it is, okay?"

"Doug Campton."

Doug was one of those guys who must have been starved for attention as a child and was thus making up for it now by being a class clown. If something stupid happened at Pullman High, chances were Doug was involved. His last escapade involved his stealing the school-mascot outfit—a greyhound that actually looked more like a giant, happy rat. He put on the outfit, along with a bikini top and a hula skirt, and then ran through the gym during a home basketball game. He was carrying a sign that not only insulted the entire female population of PHS but also questioned our shaving habits.

Totally juvenile.

I gathered a few books in one arm. "Tell Doug, I'd rather just be friends."

Logan, who hasn't ever taken an interest in my love life other than to make fun of whom I'm dating, looked disappointed. "Oh, come on. Why don't you give him a chance?"

"Why?"

Logan shrugged and held out one hand. "I like the guy, and for some reason he likes you. I just want you both to be happy."

"No, really. Why?"

He was silent for a moment, as though debating what to say next. "All right, I'll tell you. Doug has this cousin who lives in Moscow. Veronica." Logan said her name as though savoring the word. "Her family came to watch him play the last baseball game, and I met her. She was really nice, and well, Doug says he can set me up with her if I set him up with you."

"Why don't you just call Veronica yourself?" Moscow, Idaho, is only eight miles away from Pullman, and even though Pullman is in Washington, the cities are so close together and both so small, we use the same phone book.

"I don't know her last name, and Doug won't tell me. It's blackmail, and I need your help. Come on, Samantha, you go out with everybody. What difference would it make if you go out with Doug? Just one date with him, that's all I'm asking."

Logan had never asked me for a favor before. I enjoyed the moment and smiled over at him graciously. "You know, I was in a bad mood when I came in, and I have to thank you for doing your part to bring me out of it. Really, it's so gratifying to know I have the power to make you happy or miserable. I feel much better now."

"I'll take your next weekend shift for you."

"Not a chance." I ran a finger over the books in the cart, checking a last time for any that might be in my section.

"The next two."

"Nope."

"All right, you tell me what it would take. What do you want from me?"

It was ironic he should offer to help me now, when I needed help so badly. If Logan could have somehow made my SAT scores go up, I would have jumped at the chance. But he couldn't do that. No one could. I suppose I could have asked him to help me study for the entire next year, but he wouldn't have agreed to that.

I sighed dejectedly. "Sorry, what I want, you can't get me."

Logan blinked at me, his eyebrows raised in a question. He probably thought I was talking about some sort of criminal activity. In a mildly shocked voice he said, "And what exactly would that be?"

"Better grades."

"Oh. Well, you're right there." He paused for a moment and then added, "Since when did you start caring about your grades?"

"Since I started thinking about college."

"Ahh, I guess that cheerleading scholarship didn't come through, huh?"

"No, and I suppose you're still waiting for your application to comedian school."

"Naw, I'm going to Western Washington University."

WWU. That was one of the schools I'd been considering. You'd think that knowing Logan was going there would have made WWU seem less desirable, but it had the opposite effect. I absolutely couldn't be rejected by a place that Logan could be so casual about getting into.

"Are you sure you have the grades to get in?" I asked.

He shrugged. "I think so. And besides, they take other factors into consideration when they review your application. I've been in student body council for years." He smiled over at me nonchalantly. "I've got leadership qualities."

"And so many other qualities too—many of which I have to endure on a daily basis. Do they take those into consideration too?"

Logan laughed then, which was something else I found annoying. One moment he'd be so spiteful I'd want to slap him, and the next moment he'd smile over at me like we were the best of friends.

"If you go out with Doug, I promise never to annoy you again."

"That's a promise you can't keep." I walked over to the general fiction section with the rest of my books, and this time Logan didn't follow me. I knew he hadn't given up on this whole Doug thing, though. He'd probably be bugging me for days, until I was so frustrated with it all I'd have to drive to Moscow and go on a door-to-door search for Veronica myself.

Still, I wasn't mad at Logan. In fact, for the first time in the shift I was in a good mood because he'd given me an idea. As soon as Logan mentioned leadership qualities, I mulled it over. Why couldn't I do something that would show my leadership qualities too? I had them, after all. As head cheerleader, I was constantly organizing things. All I had to do was show colleges that I was a leader. And the election for next year's school officers was less than a month away.

When I got home from work, I kept the envelope with my SAT scores in my purse and didn't mention to my parents that they'd come. I wasn't exactly sure what their reaction to a score of 810 would be, but I had a vague fear it might be grounding me until I reached that same age.

The lecturing would go on all night.

Dad: Young lady, you obviously need to spend more time on your studies. Don't come out of your room until you can calculate the square root of pi in your head.

Me: But—

Mom: And no more dating until you're a straight-A student.

Dad: That's right. We've never liked the guys you hang around with, and this gives us the perfect excuse to banish them from your life. From here on out, we decree that any guys who are cute, cool, or listen to music with lyrics we can't understand won't be allowed to cross our threshold.

Me: But—

Mom: And while we're angry I'd like to point out that your room is a mess, you haven't practiced the piano in weeks, and you're two inches shorter than I've always wanted you to be.

Me: But—

Dad: And stop calling us names. You're grounded.

Okay, maybe my parents wouldn't be that extreme. Well, at least my dad wouldn't be. Mom tended to get worked up easily. She expected me to do everything flawlessly. Apparently the SAT was one area where I was far from flawless.

I'd have to tell my parents eventually, but I could put it off as long as possible.

The next day at school I decided I would definitely run for office. Then I decided I definitely wouldn't. As I watched all the people passing me in the hallways, I asked myself, *Would they vote for me?* Did enough people think I could do the job—did enough people *like* me—to elect me? I hoped so, but I knew there might also be a very painful answer to this question. Did I really want to find out?

I didn't mention the possibility of my candidacy to anyone that day. I told myself I'd talk with my friends about it the next day, but somehow I never got around to mentioning it then, either.

Finally, I decided the best place to test-drive the idea was on my date with Brad. He would understand how I felt. Perhaps he'd even murmur words of encouragement to me.

He came to pick me up at five so we could go to dinner before we saw a movie. When the doorbell rang, I was in the middle of taking out my hot curlers, so I sent my mom to the door before one of my little brothers could get it. I have three younger brothers: Andy, who's seven, and the twins, Joe and David, who are ten—all of whom are major pains. They seem to think anything female is hilarious and have no qualms about sharing aspects of my beauty regime with any guy who walks in the door.

"She puts this thick, gooey clay stuff on her face every night," they told my last boyfriend. "You'll be sorry if you marry her."

So I sent my mom to answer the door. Which turned out to be a mistake. While I was unrolling my curls she started discussing the evening plans with Brad.

Maybe the problem is I date too much. If I hardly ever went out, then my mom would be nervously trying to impress my dates in order to encourage them. As it is, my mom sees the guys in my life as something between an annoyance ("Okay kids, Samantha's got a guy coming to pick her up in fifteen minutes, so get your stuff off the living-room floor before I throw it away!") and an unlimited resource ("So, Bryce, I hear your father is an orthodontist. Would he mind looking at Joe's teeth sometime?").

Today when I walked into the living room, Brad stood beside my mom with a trapped expression on his face, and I knew he'd become a resource.

Mom scooped up our nine-month-old tabby cat from the couch and smiled over at me. "Brad tells me you're going to El Marcado. That's just a hop, skip, and a jump away from the animal clinic."

"I'm sure it's perfectly sanitary anyway," I said, grabbing my jacket from the hall closet and slipping my purse over my shoulder.

Mom ignored me. "And you know I'm supposed to take Frisky in tonight to be spayed. It would really be great if you could drop her off for me."

"You want me to take the cat on our date?"

"Not on your date. Just to the vet's office. It's on the way to the restaurant."

I shifted my purse on my shoulder, fiddling with the strap as I inched toward the front door. "Won't the clinic be closed by now?"

"They stay open until nine."

At this point Andy wandered into the living room and started tugging on Mom's shirt to get her attention.

"Don't take Frisky away," he whined. "We want her to have kittens."

"No, we don't," Mom said.

"But kittens are so cute!" he said.

"Sure, they're cute when they're kittens, but they grow up to be cats. So Samantha and Brad are taking Frisky to the vet."

I put my hand on the doorknob and sent her a pleading look. "Mom . . ." *Please don't make me do this. And please don't start an argument in front of Brad. I'm trying to look mature, sophisticated, and just a little bit glamorous. Hauling a cat around with me is not a way to accomplish any of these goals.*

Mom apparently has no telepathic powers. While she went on about how it wouldn't be "any trouble at all" and how she'd taken Frisky in for shots three weeks ago and the cat "behaved perfectly fine," she handed Frisky to Brad.

Brad stood there, frozen, holding the cat slightly away from his sweater, eyeing her like she might have fleas.

I knew he didn't want to even hold the cat, let alone chauffeur her to the vet's, but he was too polite to hand her back to my mom. Which is why, I suppose, Mom handed Frisky to Brad instead of to me.

"Thanks, dear," Mom said. She took Andy's hand and headed toward the kitchen. "I have so many other things to do, and this saves me a trip." Over her shoulder she called out, "Have fun at dinner," and then disappeared into the kitchen.

I reached over and took Frisky from Brad's arms. "Sorry about this."

"It's okay."

I knew it wasn't. My telepathic powers apparently work much better than my mother's, and I could tell Brad would rather have stitches than carry our cat around. So I would hold her, and we'd just try to get the feline-escorting part of the evening over as quickly as possible.

We walked out to Brad's car, and I absentmindedly stroked Frisky's gray fur to let her know that everything was fine. Her name is a misnomer. She was only frisky for the first two months of her kittenhood. Immediately thereafter she became lazy, slothful, and a whole slew of less-than-cute adjectives, but by then it was too late to change her name. Besides, she probably wouldn't answer to Lays-on-the-couch-licking-her-fur.

I climbed into Brad's car and set Frisky down on the seat beside me while I put on my seat belt. Brad got in on the other side and kept sending Frisky sideways glances while he fastened his own belt. I could tell he was wondering how much cat hair she shed per minute, so I picked her up and put her back on my lap. True, I would probably spend the rest of our date looking like I was wearing furry jeans, but better to look funny than to have your date upset because you'd messed up his upholstery.

Brad turned on the ignition, and Frisky's claws came out. I calmly tried to peel her off my jeans without screaming. Screaming probably wouldn't help soothe a nervous cat.

"It's okay, Frisky," I breathed out. "We're just taking you on a trip to the vet."

"Where they'll cut you open and remove parts of your body," Brad added.

"You're not helping."

"It's not like she can understand English."

Frisky peered out the window, her eyes darting back and forth at the scenery, and she let out a long, low meow. Not like the cute little *myerts* she uses when she wants food. This sounded more like a gravelly, possessed can opener.

"Is she all right?" Brad asked, taking his eyes off the road for longer than I liked.

"I'm sure she'll be fine. Just hurry."

He sped up. A lot.

"Not that fast."

He didn't slow down. "I thought your mother said the cat traveled just fine when she went in for her shots."

"Well, maybe Frisky remembers that the last time she went for a car ride she got stuck by a bunch of sharp needles."

The speed did nothing to soothe Frisky. She leaped from my lap and prowled back and forth in the car, searching for a way out. Every once in a while she bellowed her gravelly meows at us.

"Would you get her off the dashboard," Brad hissed. "It's hard to drive when I'm waiting for her to pounce on the steering wheel."

I reached over to grab her, but she sprang from the dashboard to the top of the seat. While I twisted around trying to pry her from there, she let out another series of possessed sounding *me-ee-ow-ows*.

"Is she clawing my car seats?" Brad asked.

"No. I mean, not on purpose."

Brad muttered something under his breath and pressed down on the gas pedal. Street signs and mailboxes zipped past us.

"I think you're scaring her." *And if not her, than certainly me.* I tried to get hold of Frisky, and Frisky tried to hide by wedging herself in between my back and the seat of the car. I leaned forward so I could reach back and grab her, but she kept moving farther down my back. I didn't know whether to be relieved or not that her claws were facing me, and not Brad's precious upholstery.

Brad took his eyes off the road again to look over at me. "What is she doing now?"

"I don't know. I don't speak cat."

Luckily, we made it downtown and Brad had to slow the car for the lights and the traffic. He kept glancing over at me, perhaps waiting to see if the cat was going to explode or something.

Frisky, discovering there was no way to dig out through the seat, turned around and began crawling up my back. I attempted to gain control of the situation by repeating, "Frisky, stop that!" over and over again while I tried to grab something that was neither claws nor teeth.

I finally got hold of her, but she wouldn't sit in my lap. This time she crawled up the front of my shirt, stopped for a moment to stand on my shoulder, and then latched on to my head, like it was the top of Mount Everest.

While he was waiting for the light to turn green Brad glanced over at me. "The frisky cat is on your head!"

Actually, I'm not sure *frisky* was the adjective he used, but the word definitely began with an *F.*

"I realize the cat is on my head."

"People are staring at us."

I had been too busy trying to pull the cat off of various parts of my body to pay attention to the other cars around us, but now I looked. The car next to us carried several teenage boys, all of whom stared openmouthed at me. Their mouths were open, I assume, because they were laughing too hard to shut them.

I slunk farther down in the seat and ripped Frisky off my hair. She clawed my ear in the process. I wanted to toss her in the backseat like a shot put, but before I did, I noticed her mouth. It had bubbles of saliva all around it. Still holding her midway in the air, I said, "Brad, I think she's sick."

"Not in my car!"

She was going to throw up. I knew she was going to throw up, and I sat there holding her, trying to figure out which direction to point her. Did I want to get cat vomit all over me or all over Brad's car?

The thought of half-digested Tender Vittles—or worse yet, some mangled mouse corpse—was more than I could imagine wearing. Even to save Brad's upholstery.

Brad was watching Frisky so intently he didn't notice the light turn green, and the car behind us honked.

Which did nothing to help Frisky's fragile mental condition.

Besides digging her claws into my arms, she made gagging noises.

"Don't let her throw up," Brad said.

And exactly how was I supposed to stop that from happening? Tell her to take deep, soothing breaths? Roll down the window and tell her to hang her head out? If I rolled down the window, she would have been out of the car faster than I could say, "You don't really have nine lives." Then I'd have to go home and explain to my little brothers how Frisky had been flattened into a kitty pancake by the oncoming traffic. So, instead, I just held her, watching the bubbles of saliva around her mouth grow until they dripped onto my jeans. I looked around for something to wipe her mouth with. Did I have Kleenex in my purse?

"She's foaming at the mouth!" Brad said.

"Would you please watch the traffic instead of the cat?"

"Isn't that something rabid animals do before they bite you?"

"She can't have rabies. My mom just took her in for her shots three weeks ago."

"Maybe the shot didn't have time to work."

I set Frisky on my lap and reached for the Kleenex in my purse. The saliva had already dripped all over me, so now along with cat hair I also had cat spit covering me. The perfect thing to complete my ensemble.

"What are you doing?" Brad asked. "Don't let a rabid animal loose in my car!"

"She isn't rabid. And I'm trying to get something to wipe off her mouth."

Frisky didn't stay to let me wipe off her mouth. While I was still fishing Kleenex squares out of my purse she jumped into the backseat.

Brad peered over the seat at her, swerving the car toward the shoulder as he did. "Now your cat is drooling all over my car. This is great. Just great. I'm stuck in a car with a *rabid, drooling cat!*"

"You know, at this point I think your chances of being killed in a reckless car accident are a lot greater than being attacked by a rabid cat. So why don't you just *watch where you're going!*"

And that's how it was when we pulled up to the vet's

office. We were yelling at each other about how we were going to die.

Brad and I got out of the car, and I opened the door closest to the cat. Frisky was huddled in the crevice under the driver's seat, and I wasn't sure whether she'd thrown up or simply drooled back there. I wasn't about to put my hand under the seat to find out. I tried to change the tone of my voice from the yelling-at-Brad tone to the here-kitty-I'm-really-your-friend tone.

"Come on out, Frisky," I cooed. "Everything is just fine now. There's nothing to be afraid of."

Frisky didn't buy it.

Apparently there was nothing amiss about *her* telepathic powers, and she was not about to let us haul her into the animal clinic.

"Come here, Frisky," I said again.

Brad stood behind me, looking over my shoulder. "Just reach down there and grab her."

Oh, sure. He was standing there with his hands in his pockets, but he wanted me to grab the angry, rabid cat. That's chivalry for you.

I reached down cautiously, more afraid of upchucked mice than of being bitten, but before I could even touch Frisky, she shot past me out of the open door.

"Get her!" I yelled to Brad.

But Brad didn't have time to reach her even if he wanted to, which I'm pretty sure he didn't. I could tell by the way his hands were still in his pockets and the way he looked not at the cat, but at the backseat of his car.

I wouldn't have thought Frisky capable of such a burst of energy, but in seconds she'd sprinted across the sidewalk, jumped from a garbage can to a tree, to the roof of the vet's office. Once there, she sat glaring down at us from behind the rain gutter.

"Now what are we going to do?" I moaned.

"I don't know what *we* are going to do, but *I* am going to take my car home and clean it out. It smells funny, and who knows what that psycho cat of yours did underneath my seat."

"You're going to leave me here with my cat stuck on the roof?"

"What do you want me to do? Climb up there after her? Maybe I could break my neck just to make the evening complete." He flung open the car door and jumped into the driver's seat. "I've got to get rid of this smell before it becomes permanent."

He slammed the door shut and screeched out of the parking lot.

"Jerk," I called after him. "Jerk! Jerk! *Jerk!*"

Then I glared back up at the cat. "And you're a jerk too! It isn't enough that you wake me up every morning by stepping on my face—now you're ruining my love life! I ought to—"

I stopped my tirade when I realized several people in the parking lot had just gotten out of their cars, and they were now all staring at the crazed teenager who was yelling, for some indiscernible reason, at the side of a building.

Without another glance at Frisky, I walked into the clinic and explained, in a surprisingly coherent manner, the situation to the receptionist.

She shrugged sympathetically, but didn't move away from the desk. "We don't have a ladder here, but usually cats will come down if you coax them long enough."

Right. I was supposed to stand out on the sidewalk for

who knew how long, looking like an idiot, while I tried to reason with a cat.

I walked back outside. Frisky was calmly surveying the parking lot from her rain gutter, with no apparent intention of ever coming down. I uttered a few more threats at her, then pulled my cell phone from my purse and called home. Let Mom deal with the cat crisis. I just wanted to go somewhere where I could wipe the cat spit off my jeans. Besides, she needed to come pick me up anyway, since Brad had left me stranded at the vet's office.

Jerk.

Mom answered the phone. I wanted her to be sorry—no, mortified—for what had happened, for what she'd caused to happen. Instead, she just sounded irritated.

"Frisky is on the roof? Why did you let her do that?"

"I didn't *let* her. I didn't give her my permission. Not once did I ever tell her it was a good idea. *You* should try catching a neurotic, terrified cat."

Mom sighed. "I'll be right down." Then she hung up.

I waited for her on the sidewalk, every once in a while glancing up at Frisky. I wanted to yell at her some more, but didn't dare. One can only endure so many strangers thinking you're insane, and I'd already passed my quota.

Finally Mom pulled up in our minivan. She stepped out, ignored me, and walked to the side of the building. "Frisky, it's dinnertime."

The cat meowed once—one of its normal *myerts,* not the possessed-sounding kind she'd been using on me, then leaped down from the roof.

Mom scooped her up and gave her a scratch underneath the chin. "Sorry to lie," she told the cat, "but you can't have anything to eat until after your surgery." Then Mom turned to me. "See, that wasn't really so hard, was it?"

I stared at her, just stared at her for a long moment. "Mom, you know how every once in a while when you want to point out how grateful I ought to be to have you as a mother, you tell me about how you were in labor for eighteen hours with me?"

"Yes."

"Well, I think I can trump that now. The next time you tell me all about childbirth pains, I'm going to tell you about the time you made me take the cat to the vet, and I was humiliated, clawed, drooled on, and spent a portion of the car ride wearing a rabid cat on my head."

"Frisky can't be rabid, dear. She's had her shots."

"I don't care!" I yelled. "I hate her anyway!"

Mom stroked the cat gently, as though realizing for the first time what a traumatic experience Frisky must have had. I stomped off to the van, but I still heard her anyway, softly telling the cat, "Don't be too upset about the procedure, Frisky. Trust me, you don't want children. Sure, they're cute when they're babies, but they grow up to be teenagers."

When we got back home, I went straight to the bathroom and put antiseptic on my cat scratches. I wished I had something to put on my other wounds, but they don't bottle anything to put on humiliation. Or disappointment. Or fear that a guy is going to tell all of his friends you spent the evening covered in cat drool.

The vet told us as he slipped Frisky into a cage that cats often foam at the mouth when they're nervous. Which was a cat fact I hadn't previously known. What an informative day it had turned out to be. I'd tell Brad about it if I ever spoke to him again.

Why was it every time I started to like a guy things always turned out miserably? Was it really so much to ask that a guy act considerate? Understanding? Responsible enough not to drive his car like it was an airborne vehicle?

I expected Brad to call me sometime over the weekend. He didn't. I wish guys would let you know why they don't call. It would have made my life so much easier if I knew whether he hadn't called because (a) he'd decided that even the chance of spending any more time in the vicinity of me or my upchucking cat was too risky; (b) he was ashamed of the way he'd yelled at me, cursed my pet, and left me stranded at the animal clinic, and was now thinking of the perfect way to beg my forgiveness; or (c) there were some really good games on ESPN he had to watch.

By the time Monday came, I still didn't know how to feel and couldn't think about anything else.

I drove to school earlier than normal to make sure I had plenty of time to discuss the matter of Brad with my friends. Every morning before classes started, I got together with Rachel, Chelsea, and Aubrie. We had all been cheerleading together since our freshman year, and even though basketball season was now over, we still got together every morning by the main landing to watch people go by.

Rachel insisted on it, in fact. She had to get her senior-stud ogling in for the day. Chelsea specialized in ogling too, but she watched everyone so she could critique their outfits. She planned on becoming a fashion designer, so it was good professional practice for her.

Aubrie and I just stood on the landing for the company, but I helped Chelsea with her fashion critiques.

"Crystal's striped shirt is bold, and the nautical pants definitely make a statement," Chelsea would say.

"Yes, but that statement is 'Please throw me overboard,' " I'd add.

"Although Ashley's shirt is the right color for her skin tone, it's about two sizes too tight."

"But on the plus side, if she's ever bleeding to death, it can double as a tourniquet."

Generally we'd end up laughing so hard people would start looking at us suspiciously as they went by, and then we'd have to do our critiques in a whisper.

But today as we leaned against the banister in the lobby my friends debated whether guys or pets were easier to handle.

"Pets are more loyal," Rachel said.

"But you don't have to worry about guys throwing up in your car," Aubrie countered.

"Unless they've been drinking," Chelsea said.

"Yeah, do you remember when Darren drank like half a keg and then got sick at the homecoming dance?" Rachel shuddered. "I *wish* he'd been in his car instead of trying to run off the dance floor."

"Another point in pets' favor," Aubrie said. "They know how to hold their liquor."

"Back to the subject of Brad," I said. "We're supposed to go to the prom, but I don't even know if we're still on speaking terms. I mean, what am I going to do about that?"

Chelsea tilted her chin. "It's a little late to find another date. The dance is less than three weeks away. You'll just have to swallow your pride and make up with him."

"You can still have a good time," Aubrie added. "Just don't bring your cat along."

I smirked as I imagined Frisky wedged between Brad and me in our prom pictures.

"Guys smell better than animals," Chelsea said.

"Not always. It depends on the guy," Rachel said.

"Guys are better kissers."

"That also depends on the guy," Rachel said.

Aubrie cocked her head. "*Who* have you been kissing?"

Rachel giggled obscenely. Rachel is just that way.

Chelsea folded her arms and got a faraway look on her face. "Wouldn't it be poetic justice if Brad got sick from drinking on prom night and threw up in his own car?"

"He'd better not be drinking on prom night," I said. "I've seen how he drives when he's sober."

"Lassie would have never left Samantha stranded in a parking lot," Aubrie said. "I think pets win."

"A boyfriend would never have scaled a wall and sat on the vet's roof in the first place," Chelsea said.

"He would if he knew the vet was trying to fix him," Rachel said.

Then all of my friends laughed and started suggesting the positive attributes of neutering.

"Okay, forget the subject of veterinary procedures," I said, and plunged into a subject change before I had to listen to any more anatomy talk. "School elections are a week after prom. Have any of you ever thought of running for anything?"

Rachel shrugged, and her gaze returned to the river of students that made its way across the lobby. "Not really. Why?"

"I was just thinking that it looked like a lot of fun."

Chelsea snorted. "What part do you think is fun? Planning things with the teachers? Like I don't already see enough of them."

"I wasn't talking about that part," I said. "I just mean, you know, being a leader."

"Leading cheers is enough for me, and it's not like we even got a lot of thanks for that." Rachel folded her arms. "You know those cookies we always bake for the team? I think a total of one person has ever said thank you to me."

Aubrie nodded. "Guys don't say thank you. That's why, in the end, they all get married—to have someone write their thank-you cards for them."

"And to have someone pick out clothes for them to wear every day," Chelsea added. "What is it with the Y chromosome that prohibits them from matching colors?"

"That's another point in favor of pets," Rachel said. "They never wear stupid clothes."

I tried to steer the conversation back to me. "But being in the student body council could be fun, don't you think?"

Aubrie leaned back against the banister and shot me a suspicious glance. "Are you thinking of running for something?"

I didn't answer right away. For a second longer I could change my mind and back out. For a second longer I didn't have to worry about planning, campaigning, or, more importantly, losing. "Yeah, I think I'll run for president."

"President?" Chelsea asked.

"Yes, president." I figured if I was going for leadership potential, then I had better run for president. I'm not sure how much stock universities put in secretaries or vice presidents.

Rachel winked over at Aubrie. "I think someone had better tell Samantha that high school presidents don't get interns."

"Or the power to nuke other high schools," Chelsea added.

I glared at Rachel and Chelsea.

"What?" Rachel said. "You're not serious, are you?"

"Why wouldn't I be?"

She bit back a smile. "Because you're the one who's always said student government was for people who didn't have the talent to do sports or the rhythm to do cheerleading. Did you suddenly lose your rhythm?"

"No, I suddenly got my SAT scores." I hadn't meant to tell them my reasoning, but none of them looked shocked. In a quieter voice I added, "I thought my college application might need a boost, like a term as school president."

Everyone was silent for a moment, then Aubrie said, "So how bad was your score?"

"Eight ten."

Chelsea winced. "Well, you might have rhythm, but apparently you don't have math or English skills."

"I'll do better next year on them, but I still think it would be a good idea if I ran for student body president too. You guys will help me campaign, won't you?"

"Sure," Rachel said. "We can help you. What do you need? Posters? Flyers? Nasty rumors about your opponents?"

"I don't want to spread rumors about anyone. That wouldn't be fair."

Chelsea let out a half grunt. "Fair? This is politics. You have to do whatever it takes to win."

"I am going to do what it takes. And right now I think it will take posters. Are you guys going to help me or not?"

"Posters we can do," Aubrie said, and then they spent the rest of the time until the bell rang discussing possible campaign slogans.

I nodded every once in a while, but I was only half paying attention. Chelsea's words still hung in the air before me, and I couldn't see beyond them. You have to do whatever it takes to win. What did she think it was going to take?

Brad had the same lunch hour as I did, and he usually stopped by my table to talk with me. I wondered if he would show up today and what he'd say.

I wanted to give him another chance; giving him another chance would be easier than breaking up. I could even forget being stranded in the parking lot if he'd just apologize. With sincerity.

But Brad never showed up. I saw him only once, across the cafeteria. He walked out without even looking in my direction.

I went to my English class and fumed about Brad while I was supposed to be listening to a lesson on the passive voice. I kept thinking about the prom. Would Brad and I make up by then, or would the evening be just one long, uncomfortable ordeal interspersed with dancing? Should I be the one to try to smooth things over? Did I even want to go to the prom with Brad? I debated this question instead of listening to the lecture on the proper use of semicolons.

Which would be worse: swallowing my pride and acting like everything had been my fault—and then having to put up with a boyfriend who thought it was—or spending prom night with someone I was barely speaking to? What great dance pictures *that* would produce.

After school, while I took my books out of my locker Chelsea walked up. She put one hand on my locker door and leaned closer to me. "Did you hear about Brad and Whitney?"

"No, what about them?"

"He asked her to the prom."

I stood, openmouthed, waiting for Chelsea to tell me she was kidding. But she didn't.

Finally I turned back to my locker. "Well, it was nice of him to inform me we weren't going, before he asked someone else."

"Total loser," Chelsea agreed. "You're better off without him."

"Sure." She was right, but it didn't seem like much consolation after being dumped in such a nasty manner. I swallowed hard to try to keep my throat from tightening. I absolutely was not going to cry about this. He wasn't worth it.

Chelsea leaned up against the locker next to mine. "I say, tonight we go out, find every stray cat in the city, and put them all in Brad's car."

"That would be cruel. To the cats, I mean."

"Better yet, you should tell Brad it turns out Frisky really did have rabies, and now his upholstery is infected with dangerous germs."

I smiled, but just a little. "And the car needs to be demolished for safety reasons."

"Right. He and Whitney can walk to the prom."

I shoved the last of my books into my backpack. "We'd be doing Whitney a favor. She'd be much safer that way."

"You can find another date for the prom. You'll go with a better guy."

"Right." And who would that be? It was three weeks till the dance, and most people already had their plans set. My stomach knotted up. I had to go. I'd already bought my dress and shoes. I was on the prom committee. How could I help decorate the place and then not go to the event?

I said my good-byes to Chelsea and walked slowly out of the school to the parking lot to find my car.

I could always go with Doug.

No. I wasn't that desperate. After all, Doug would probably show up for the prom in the greyhound outfit.

There was Logan.

I groaned out loud and flung open my car door. Why had his name popped into my mind when I was thinking of prom dates? Logan and I couldn't get along for one evening, even if we *both* were desperate. He'd probably rather eat staples than go out with me. *I* would rather eat staples.

So who?

I climbed into my car and took a deep breath to calm down. Someone would ask me. They had to. How could I even contemplate being popular enough to run for president if I wasn't popular enough to be asked to the prom?

This thought haunted me for the rest of the day.

On Tuesday I talked, flirted, and smiled my most upbeat smiles to all the cute guys in my classes. Upbeat shows you have confidence. Upbeat shows you don't care if some guy just dumped you.

At lunchtime, while I put my books in my locker, Brad walked up to me. He leaned up against the locker next to mine, just like it had been any other day.

"I wanted to talk to you about the prom . . ."

"Did you? Are you sure you didn't want to talk to Whitney about the prom?"

I slammed my locker door and faced him square on. "Why don't you just tell her whatever it was you wanted to say, and let it get back to me through the grapevine. That worked so well last time."

A tinge of red rose in Brad's neck. "Sorry, but after the way you were yelling at me on Friday—"

"Oh. The way I was yelling at you on Friday? That's nothing compared to the way I'm going to be yelling at you in two seconds."

Apparently two seconds was too long for him to stick around. He mumbled something under his breath, questioned which species I belonged to, then turned and walked down the hallway.

"Loser!" I called after his retreating back. "You are such a lowlife, Brad!"

It was then that I noticed Logan and a couple of his friends walking up the hallway, witnesses to the scene I'd just made. Logan raised an eyebrow, then turned back to his friends. As they walked by me he said in a louder-than-normal voice, "And the really amazing thing is, that's the way Samantha talks to guys she *likes*."

I didn't set him straight.

When I got home from school, I found Mom in the kitchen kneading a bowlful of bread dough. She took a French cooking class once a week, so every Tuesday she'd present us with some strange and exotic dish for dinner. Then we'd all have to pretend we were really full, and not just too uncultured to appreciate stuffed veal kidneys.

Bread looked normal, though. I walked farther into the kitchen, eyeing the counter for rogue ingredients she might be planning to ruin the bread with. No sign of escargot, truffle paste, or liver pâté.

Mom punched the dough, and puffs of flour floated up into the air. "Samantha, my hands are sticky. Would you get the butter out of the fridge?"

Butter was good. Part of a regular food group. I got it out of the refrigerator and put it on the counter by her. "What are you making?"

"Croissants."

"Great. I love croissants."

"They're for the goose-neck-and-garlic sandwiches."

"Goose neck? People actually eat that on purpose? I always

thought that was one of those animal by-products that ended up in dog food."

Mom wiped a section of hair that had fallen into her face, leaving a smear of flour across her cheek. "Goose neck is a delicacy. You have to at least try it. In fancy restaurants people pay up to fifty dollars a plate for this stuff."

And at our house we were force-fed it for free. Just another irony of life.

I waited until Mom was spreading flour over the counter, then grabbed a bagel from the bread box. I surreptitiously took a bite, then inched toward the kitchen door. She plopped down the croissant dough on the counter and asked, "Did anything good come in the mail?"

"Not unless we've actually won the Publishers Clearinghouse Sweepstakes this time."

"Your SAT scores didn't come today?"

"No." Technically it wasn't a lie. They didn't come *today*.

Mom got out the rolling pin and flattened the dough into a circle. "I talked to Linda Benson today. She said Elise got her test score—a composite of twelve hundred. Can you believe it?"

Elise was a girl my age whose bad attitude canceled out all of her good looks. Elise said and did whatever she wanted, including—and especially—tormenting anyone who got on her bad side. Last year we went to the same girls' camp, and she averaged two practical jokes a day—three if you counted the ones she played on the leaders. If she wasn't sewing someone's tent flap shut, she was hiding plastic bugs in the sleeping bags. I fell victim to her jokes on a daily basis. My shampoo was dyed orange, my sleeping bag wandered by itself to tents across the camp several times, and one morning I woke up with purple marker lines across my cheeks. Everyone called me Poca-Samantha for the rest of camp.

All of this wouldn't have been so bad if Elise actually got in trouble for any of it, but no one ever caught her. I knew she was guilty, though. I could tell by the way she smirked innocently every time it happened.

Anyway, I wouldn't have thought Elise cared enough about school to be able to count to 1200, let alone get that score on the SAT. I actually pay attention in class most of the time, and I got an 810. Life is so unfair.

Mom said, "Don't worry about your scores. I'm sure you did great. I just wish they were here already so I could start bragging about you."

No, I thought, *you really don't.*

"I bet they come tomorrow."

I'd take that bet. In fact, I'd bet they were never going to come. They'd been inexplicably lost in the mail. Perhaps even rerouted to a small village in Albania. Funny how those things happened sometimes.

I decided to change the subject. "Class elections are coming up. I thought I'd run for president."

Mom spread a thin slab of butter across the dough, then folded it over. "That's wonderful. You'll make a great president."

"Well, I have to win first."

"Who's going to be your vice president?"

"Whoever the student body votes for. We don't run as a ticket."

Mom spun the rolling pin across the dough again and shook her head. "That's not very efficient. What if you and the vice president have opposite political views?"

"I think mostly we just plan dances, fund-raisers, that sort of thing."

"You should still have some sort of an agenda. What are you planning to campaign on?"

"Poster boards. Flyers. Maybe some buttons if they're not too expensive."

"I meant what issues are you campaigning on?"

Issues? What was the point of having issues when all you did was plan dances and fund-raisers? I imagined myself standing in front of the student body delivering my campaign speech. "And if elected, I promise not to hire bands who have thus far performed only in their garages and who create songs using screeching sounds instead of actual musical notes. Furthermore, if elected, I promise that when we do our annual car wash fund-raiser, none of you will have to scrape bugs off of strangers' radiator grills. We'll make the incoming freshmen do that."

No one paid attention to issues. I shrugged. "I'll probably stress school unity."

Mom made a low *hmmm* sound as she refolded the dough, which meant she didn't like school unity as an issue and was about to launch into a speech about politics, campaigning, or the Constitution. Maybe all three.

Or perhaps she was about to ask me to get the goose neck out of the refrigerator.

I tucked the rest of my bagel into my pocket, said, "Well, I'd better start on my homework," and retreated from the kitchen as quickly as I could.

. . .

The next day as I headed to my first-period art class, I decided to start recruiting for my campaign. Particularly I wanted to recruit Cassidy Woodruff. She hung around with the honors crowd, and I needed an in with that group. I was sure the smart kids actually voted.

Cassidy lived down the street from me, and we'd played together a lot when we were little. We grew apart as we got older, and then last year we'd had a major falling out.

It seems whenever I fight with someone, it's over guys, and this was no exception. When Elise Benson first moved to Pullman at the beginning of our sophomore year, Cassidy and I both competed for her older brother, Josh.

And Cassidy won.

It didn't matter that Cassidy went out of her way to be nice to me afterward or even that she wrote me a note telling me she wanted us to be friends. It still had bothered me every time I saw Cassidy and Josh hanging out together at school. Every time I walked by them, I felt like Cassidy was thinking, *I'm better than Samantha. That's why she didn't get Josh. She's just second-best.*

It was a relief when Josh graduated, went to college, and I didn't have to see the two of them everywhere I went.

I strolled into the art room and picked up my half-finished collage from the storage room. Cassidy and Elise already sat at their usual table in the corner, collages, pictures, and words cut from magazine articles spread out in front of them.

You wouldn't have thought Cassidy and Elise would even get along, let alone be best friends, but they were. Elise was—well—Elise, and Cassidy was completely wholesome and sweet. If the school yearbook had a category for it, I'm sure Cassidy would be voted the girl most likely to have her likeness stamped on apple-pie boxes. She was cheerful, friendly, and pretty enough that Josh chose her instead of me.

I had to stop thinking about that.

I walked over to Elise and Cassidy's table, clutching my pictures and scraps of magazines so they didn't fall to the floor. Despite all of last year's history, I had a good chance of getting Cassidy to work on my team. She was too nice to turn anyone down. And after the Josh incident I figured she owed me one.

I dropped my stuff onto the table, smiled, and said hello. Cassidy gave me a sort of startled hello back, and Elise just eyed me suspiciously—something which I thought was totally uncalled for, since I *do* occasionally talk to them.

I sat down anyway. No one said anything to me, so I silently arranged cheerleading stickers on my paper. We were supposed to create a collage that embodied the "essence of our life." None of us were quite sure what that meant, so we were all just pasting pictures of ourselves and things we liked onto our poster boards. Elise had added the words HOT 'N' SPICY on one corner of her collage and SUPER FLIRT on another. Typical Elise. Her pictures were all ones of herself, but almost all of Cassidy's pictures were of her new little sister, Katya.

Cassidy had been an only child until four months ago, when her family adopted a two-year-old girl from a Russian orphanage. Cassidy's mom had worn a permanent beam since they adopted Katya, and Cassidy seemed almost as beamy, so I knew what to say to her to break the ice. I cleared my throat and said, "How's your little sister these days?"

Cassidy centered a picture of Katya in bright pink pajamas on her collage. "She's doing really well. I mean, she still has her hard moments, but I think for the most part she's adjusting to American life."

Elise didn't look up from her paper. "I hate to tell you this, but those 'hard moments' have nothing to do with being an American. She's just two years old. If you think it's bad now, you're in for a surprise."

"She's really sweet most of the time," Cassidy said.

"Just wait until she finds out where you keep your makeup," Elise said.

The ice was broken, but the conversation went on about Katya.

"I'm learning lots of Russian phrases," Cassidy said. "I already know how to say, 'don't throw that,' 'come back here,' and 'please stop crying, I'll give you whatever you want.' "

"Better learn how to say, 'no, you can't borrow my clothes,' " Elise said.

I had no idea how to steer the conversation to the school election. Finally I decided for the direct approach. During the next pause in the conversation I said, "You guys have done really well on your collages. I bet you would do a great job making posters."

Both girls looked at me with puzzled expressions.

"I need to be on the lookout for people to make posters for me because I'm running for school president." I waited a moment for this information to sink in, then smiled over at them. "How about it? I'd really appreciate it if you guys worked on my campaign."

"That's really nice of you to ask us," Cassidy said, "but you know our friend Amy Stock? She told us she might run, so we'll probably help her."

"Amy Stock?" I had known I would have competition in

my bid for the presidency, but this was the first time I'd heard who. It could have been worse. Amy was the kind of girl who was friendly to everyone, but not highly popular. She wore wire-rim glasses, nondescript clothing, and an air of continual seriousness. She was smart—the type of person who teachers love to have in their class, but not necessarily the type of person who students want as their president. So I didn't panic about this news, and I didn't want to just hand over Cassidy and Elise to her side.

"Oh, come on, you guys don't really want to campaign for Amy." I turned to Cassidy, tapping my glue bottle against the table at each point I made. "Think of all we've been through together. Making snow forts, learning to roller-skate, Mr. Swenson's seventh-grade lit class. You know me much better."

Cassidy smiled at me, but it was one of those stiff, forced smiles. "Sorry, we already told Amy we'd help her out."

So much for all those things she said to me last year about wanting to be friends. I was just second-best again. I shrugged. "That's okay." Then I picked up my scissors and viciously slashed off the corners of my next picture.

Elise and Cassidy exchanged an uncomfortable glance, then went back to their collages.

I pounded a picture of my family onto one corner of my poster board. I was not going to fume. When one runs into a roadblock, one must simply look beyond it. And that's what I was going to do. I'd be nice and gracious and hope that when Cassidy and Elise were out campaigning for Amy, one or both of them would be struck mute.

Elise glued a picture of Josh with the rest of the family onto her poster board. It seemed to be a recent photo, perhaps taken right before he left Pullman.

"That's a good picture of Josh," I said. "How's he doing in college?"

"Really well."

I glanced over at Cassidy with a forced smile. "It must be hard not having him around all of the time."

Cassidy didn't look up at me. In fact, she looked quite determinedly at the Milky Way wrapper she glued next to the word CHOCOHOLIC. In an even voice she said, "Josh and I broke up."

"You broke up?" I wasn't trying to rub it in, I was genuinely surprised.

"They didn't break up," Elise said. "They just put their relationship on hold."

"We broke up," Cassidy said.

Elise rolled her eyes and sighed. Apparently they'd disagreed on this subject before. "He never said he wanted to break up with you."

"He said he thought we should date other people. That's the same thing."

"No, it's not, because he only said that so you wouldn't feel like you had to wait around for him while he's at college."

"Well, it would be a very considerate sentiment from Josh if it didn't also involve him dating half a dozen different girls."

"Because he couldn't be dating you. And besides, he's just friends with all those girls."

Cassidy put a blob of glue on her paper and then smacked a large picture of a book onto her collage. "You, of all people, shouldn't be so naive."

"Well, at least talk to him," Elise said. "He'll be home any day now, and none of those girls from college are coming with him."

I tried not to sound eager. "He'll be back soon? Why?"

"He finished classes in April. The only reason he's not home now is that he has to fix his car before it can make the drive. Josh's going to spend the summer working in my parents' store."

"That's great," I said, "I mean, that's really nice he's coming back to help your parents."

"He needs the money, and besides, I think he wants to be near Cassidy."

Cassidy rolled her eyes, but didn't say anything.

"Well, he could have just as easily gotten a job where he was," Elise told her.

"Except your parents don't own a store where he was," I said. Elise glared at me, but I ignored her and went back to working on my collage.

Josh was coming back for the summer. Dark-haired, blue-eyed, perfect Josh. Okay, he wasn't absolutely perfect. He did have Elise for a sister, but I could overlook this detail. He and Cassidy had broken up, and that meant I had a chance with him, a chance to stop being second-best.

As I sat down in the cafeteria at lunch I looked at the table where Cassidy and Elise were eating. Amy wasn't even with them. She sat at another table across the room, which just goes to show you what close friends they all were.

I tried not to think about it.

When I was halfway through my tuna-fish sandwich, Doug Campton and his friend Matt stopped by our table. Doug wore an oversized black T-shirt with a pair of baggy jeans. He looked as though he'd combed his hair sometime last week and considered that sufficient effort in the bodily care department. And Matt, well, Matt looked like a less well dressed version of Doug.

Doug stuck his hands in his pockets and tilted back on his heels. "Hey Samantha, I hear you're running for president."

"You heard right."

"Well, I hope you catch him." Both Matt and Doug laughed at this joke.

I continued to smile at them anyway. "You're going to vote for me, aren't you?"

"That depends," Matt said. "Are you going to make it worth our while?"

Suddenly I understood why people talk about politicians having no standards. As I sat there smiling at Doug and Matt,

I felt all of my standards fleeing to the lifeboats. I was not only going to have to suffer fools to win this election, I was going to have to actually pretend I liked them.

Still smiling, I said, "I think it will be worth your while to have a student body council that runs smoothly."

"Tell us more about your student body," Doug said. "I'd like to see it run smoothly."

Chelsea put her fork down on the table with a clang. "Would you also like to see her student body slap your student body?"

I laughed as though this was just pleasant banter. After all, I needed all the votes I could get. "It's great that you're interested in student council. I've organized a lot of activities over the years, but I'd really like everybody's input."

"I've got an idea," Matt said. "I think student council should throw free keggers after every game we win."

Doug shook his head. "Naw, our teams are lousy. Better just make it after every home game."

"Uh-huh," I said.

"Well, we'd better go eat lunch now," Doug said. "We just wanted to wish you luck."

"And remember the free keggers," Matt added.

After they left, I shook my head slowly. Suddenly it seemed like this election was going to take a long, long time.

Aubrie watched their retreating backs and in a lowered voice said, "Are those guys idiots, or what?"

I shrugged and took a sip of milk from my carton. "How did you expect them to turn out with names like those? *Doug* is just one *H* away from *dough,* and *mat* is something you use to wipe the mud off your feet. It's their parents who should be blamed."

Chelsea and Rachel giggled, and Aubrie swallowed a potato chip wrong and started coughing.

I leaned across the table to be closer to my friends. "Logan told me Doug wants to go out with me. What if he finds out Brad and I broke up, and he asks me to the prom?"

"Screen your calls at home," Rachel said. "And avoid him at school."

"He's not afraid to come up and talk to me," I said. "I mean, he just did."

"He wouldn't be so tacky as to ask you to the prom in front of all your friends, though," Aubrie said.

We simply stared at her for a moment, and then I said, "We're talking about Doug Campton. Tacky is part of his genetic code."

Rachel looked over at Aubrie. "The next time he comes up to us, you cause a diversion before he can talk to Samantha. Pretend to die or something."

I sighed and leaned back in my chair. "That will only work once. I just have to find another date for the prom. Fast."

I took a glance around the cafeteria. There had to be somebody decent who would like to ask me out.

Please let there be somebody.

When I walked into the bookstore after school, Logan was kneeling by a book display with a picture of a knife above it. He looked up from the mystery novels he was stacking into it and said, "You're early. What's the occasion?"

"I couldn't wait to be with you again, of course. Your charm, wit, and kindness just draw people to you."

He put the last of his books into the display. "Yeah, I know."

It occurred to me that for my campaign's sake I should attempt to be nice to Logan. Logan hung out with the smart crowd too and had a lot of friends who were potential votes. I thought this over while I checked the book cart. Nice was no good. He'd immediately know I was up to something if I was nice to him. Should I just count him as a loss, or should I strike a deal with him? If I agreed to go out with Doug once after the prom, to something really, really noncommittal, then Logan would owe me a large debt of gratitude. Exactly how much campaigning could I extract from a large debt of gratitude? Posters? Buttons? Would he perhaps agree to having VOTE FOR SAMANTHA tattooed on his forehead?

After I'd put away a batch of romances, I went and stood beside him in the western section while he shelved books. I tapped my finger over a group of book spines and waited for him to notice me. When he did, I said, "So . . . how's the world of western novels going?"

Logan raised an eyebrow at me.

"Has Zane Gray come out with anything recently?"

"Zane Gray is dead."

"Really? He sure writes a lot for a dead guy."

Logan pushed the row of books on the shelf closer together to create an opening and then tried to shove a couple of books into the space. He was only half paying attention to me.

"Um, about Doug . . . ," I said. "I might be willing to do you a favor, if you do one for me first."

Logan let the opening close and smiled. "What kind of favor?"

"I've decided to run for student body president, and I'm going to need people to help me with my campaign—"

I didn't get any further before Logan's smile turned into coughs of laughter. I glared at him while I waited for him to stop. "You could have just said no."

"It's not that I don't want to help you," he said, after more coughing. "It's just the idea of you campaigning is so funny."

"You don't think I can campaign?"

"To campaign, you have to talk to people outside your clique."

I folded my arms tightly across my chest. "I know how to be friendly."

Logan leaned toward me, using his height to make a point of looking down at me. "Samantha, you can't walk into a room of six people without insulting five of them."

"Forget I ever asked you anything. I hope you and Veronica both live long, lonely lives, and die single." I turned and walked back to the book cart with fast, long strides. Logan followed me.

"I didn't say I wouldn't campaign for you."

"And what a fine campaigner you'd be. I can just imagine your posters. VOTE FOR SAMANTHA, SHE'S SHALLOW AND INSULTING, BUT AN INTEGRAL PART OF GETTING ME A DATE. Just forget it, Logan."

I tried to take a book from the cart, but Logan held on to one end of it and wouldn't let go. He looked as though he might laugh again but was trying hard to suppress the emotion. "I'm sorry, but you have to admit it. Insulting people is your favorite pastime."

"No, it isn't." I yanked the book from his hand. "It only seems that way to you because you're so easy to insult."

"I wasn't even counting the times you insult me. If I counted those, you'd be in the Olympic insulting category."

"Logan, you're delusional." I stopped momentarily and held up my hands in mock horror. "I suppose now I've won the gold medal, haven't I?" Without waiting for his response, I picked up my books and headed to general fiction. Logan followed me. When we got there, he put one hand on the bookshelf, making it hard to ignore him. I tried anyway.

"All right," he said, "you don't agree with me. Fine. Let's see if you'll put your money where your caustic little mouth is."

"Was that an insult?" I handed him half of my books to hold while I tried to jimmy the rest onto the shelf.

"Let's make a bet of it then. I bet you can't make it through the next week without insulting someone. If I win, you'll have to go out on a date with Doug."

"And if I win?"

"Then *I'll* take you out on a date."

I took the rest of the books from his hands and gave him a patronizing stare. "That's supposed to be some big reward for me?"

"Well, I wasn't thinking of rewarding you. I was thinking more of punishing me."

I didn't insult him then, even though I wanted to, just to prove I could exercise self-control. "Fine, you'll take me to the Hilltop restaurant, where I will order lobster, *and* you'll stand on the school steps passing out flyers and telling everyone who walks by to vote for me."

Logan hesitated, but only for a moment. "All right. You have a bet."

"Fine. I won't insult anyone until"—I looked down at my watch—"four thirty-five P.M. next Wednesday, when I'll break my streak with a running commentary on your personality deficiencies. Then I'll give you flyers to hand out."

"Don't think for a minute I'll take your word about your behavior," he said. "I'm going to employ spies."

"Fine. Employ away."

Mr. Donaldson walked out of his office and looked over in our direction. I said, "Speaking of being employed . . . ," and gave Logan the we-are-being-watched look. He turned and went back to the cart, and I rearranged a few books on the shelf that someone had misplaced.

It's hard to alphabetize when you're mentally berating someone, so I replaced the books slowly. Really, Logan never ceased to amaze me. He seriously thought I'd have a hard time going a week without insulting someone. Like I have nothing better to do with my time than critique the world. I'd show him, and any and all of his spies. I would be the very model of kindness and charm for the next week. All it would take on my part was a little self-control. It would be a piece of cake—or in this case, a nice big juicy lobster.

At school on Thursday the office announced that those students interested in running for next year's executive council needed to come to the office and pick up a petition sheet. Every candidate had to get at least fifty signatures of support from fellow students. I went to the office during lunch and picked up mine.

When the secretary handed me the papers, I felt my stomach lurch. What if I couldn't find fifty people willing to sign for me? How humiliating that would be.

But then again, I'd been a cheerleader for the last three years. I'd given support, encouragement, and cookies to basketball and football players for years. They owed me. If they didn't sign my petition, then next year they'd get nothing to take on the away-game buses but burnt toast. And I'd tell them that too. In fact, I'd make it a campaign slogan.

I didn't want to walk around all day getting signatures, so I photocopied the paper and gave my friends the assignment of getting thirteen signatures each by the next day. At one point I saw Logan getting things out of his locker, and just to bother him, I went up and asked him to sign my petition. "It's only right for you to sign this," I told him, "since you'll be campaigning for me next week."

He took the paper and pen, then surveyed me skeptically. "You haven't insulted anyone today?"

"Well, only you; but it was in my mind, so it didn't count."

He tapped the pen against the paper but didn't sign it. "Hmm. Do you want to chat for a while? Tell me, who do you think is the most popular girl at PHS, and do you like her?"

I pointed to a line on the paper. "Just put your signature right there."

"Do you think Rachel is the best cheerleader in your squad, or would that have to be Aubrie?"

"It's not going to work. I'm the very essence of kindness, and I find it incredibly easy not to insult anyone."

"We'll see about that," he said, but then he signed my petition anyway.

I smiled and replaced the petition on top of my math book. "By the way, I like to order those expensive sundaes from the dessert menu."

"I'll let Doug know," he said, and turned back to his locker. Which is another annoying thing about Logan. He always has to get the last word in. When he did take me out on a date, and I made him eat every rotten word he'd ever said about me, it still probably wouldn't be an enjoyable evening. He'd find some way to ruin it. Somehow Logan would take all the fun out of gloating.

I wished him a cheerful good-bye and continued down the hallway.

I hadn't heard that Logan had asked anyone to the prom yet, and it occurred to me I could make him take me there for our date. He'd have to rent a tux, buy a corsage, and have pictures taken with me. Years hence, his children would flip through his high-school memorabilia and find his prom pictures.

"Who's that incredibly gorgeous woman you didn't have the brains to marry?" they would ask him, and then with pin-pricks of shame he'd remember me and how he'd lost our bet.

It would be fitting justice. Except it meant I would have to suffer through the prom with him, and I didn't want to do that. I only had the opportunity to go to two proms in my life. I wanted both of them to be wonderful, magical—like Cinderella going to the ball. It could never be that way if I went with Logan.

After lunch, while I got my English book out of my locker I saw Amy talking with a couple of guys. With her petition in front of her she said, "But that's the beauty of the democratic system. You can make a difference."

"Nothing ever changes," one of the guys drawled back at her. "Student council does the same stuff every year. What does it matter who wins?"

"Well, if you want a different agenda, treat this like a political race instead of a popularity contest. Vote for someone who actually knows what they're doing."

What kind of slam was that?

As if I didn't know what I was doing. Well, okay, so I didn't have any actual experience in student council, but that didn't mean I couldn't figure it out. This wasn't the Supreme Court we were talking about. This was a school election.

Amy held out a pen to the guys. I would have loved it if they'd turned her down or at least made her explain why she thought she knew what she was doing, while everyone else was a bunch of clueless dolts, but the guys just took her petition and signed it.

I refrained from slamming my locker door.

I knew what I was doing. And I wasn't about to let Amy beat me.

On Friday my friends and I stayed after school to make posters and assemble our petition lists. Since we'd made tons of posters for cheerleading, we had the whole system down to an art form. Chelsea and I did borders, die cuts, and other miscellaneous decorations. Aubrie and Rachel did lettering.

While I laid out the poster board and the other supplies I'd lugged out of my car Chelsea looked at the petitions. She shook her head as she flipped from one page to the next. "I don't believe this. Some of these morons signed more than one of our lists. What were they thinking? Like, duh, you only get one vote."

Rachel smirked at us. "Did you guys hit up the remedial students or something?"

I nearly slipped up by adding an insult of my own but closed my mouth before the words came out. Instead, I said, "Obviously, some people are very enthusiastic about voting for me."

"Well, because of their enthusiasm you now have only forty-six valid signatures instead of fifty."

"We still have time. We'll just watch for people as they walk by."

Rachel picked up one of the petition papers. "I'll go find some people."

She was entirely too eager to do this. I knew she just wanted to chat with people instead of making posters, but I didn't stop her from leaving.

Aubrie sat down cross-legged in front of one of the poster boards and pulled the lid off a marker. "Guess who else I heard is running against you, Samantha?" Without giving me time to say anything, she said, "Rick Debrock."

"Rick Debrock?" I repeated. "Why would he want to run?"

Rick was one of those rebel students whose extreme haircut matched perfectly with his strange clothes. On occasion I'd even seen him wear a safety pin through his ear. As far as I could tell, he never took school seriously, let alone showed any interest in executive council. His only concern about classes seemed to be getting through them so he could party on the weekends. Last year I had a class with him, and every Monday he came in and loudly told everyone about his weekend exploits. Most of his adventures consisted of drinking beer until he passed out.

"Rick Debrock?" I said again. "Does he have a grade point average high enough to run?"

"He must have," Aubrie said. "They gave him the paperwork. His campaign slogan is 'Party, party, party with Rick.' "

I picked up my scissors but didn't cut anything. "Do you think he'll get many votes?"

Aubrie leaned over her poster board and drew an elaborate *S*. "Most people won't take him seriously. But then again, a lot of people don't take executive council seriously, so they might vote for him just for that reason."

"He's not that wild of a guy," Chelsea said. "He just puts on the front." We both looked at her skeptically, so she added, "My sister has gone out with him a few times. He's really pretty normal outside of school."

Chelsea's little sister, Adrian, was going through what we

all called a "freak-out" stage. She seemed intent on piercing every single part of her body and had worn nothing but black for an entire year. Her going out with Rick wasn't a ringing endorsement of his normalcy.

"Well, I guess I can't count on votes from the goths, partyers, or anyone-who-hates-school-just-on-principle crowd."

"Maybe if we revamped your image a little you could appeal to those crowds." Chelsea waved her pen in my direction, as if she were a fairy godmother transforming me from a scullery maid into an acceptable candidate. "Try snarling a little, and repeat the words to all the heavy-metal songs you know."

I returned my attention to my poster. "Most people won't vote for Rick Debrock. He's probably so inebriated he can't find the school half the time, let alone try and run it."

From behind me a voice said, "Would that be an insult?"

I didn't have to turn around to tell Logan stood behind me. I clenched my teeth together. How long had he been lurking around, and more importantly, why didn't my friends tell me these sorts of things? I trimmed the corners of the poster board and kept my voice even. "That wasn't an insult. It was merely an observation."

Logan plopped his backpack on the floor and sat next to me, nearly glowing with happiness. "It sounded like an insult to me."

"Well, I suppose that's one more area in life we disagree on."

He leaned toward me and, in a voice so low only I'd hear it, said, "Stop trying to weasel out of this, you cheater. You lost our bet."

"It wasn't an insult. Rick drinks a lot. It's a substantiated fact, and one of his main campaign themes. So how can that possibly be counted as an insult? I didn't lose the bet."

I picked up a few star-shaped die cuts and glanced over at my friends. They quickly shifted their gazes from me to their posters, bending over them with intent concentration as though they weren't eavesdropping, but I knew they'd grill me about this little encounter as soon as Logan left. It was just one more ray of sunshine he was adding to my life.

Logan tapped his fingers on the floor. "I suppose it's possible you don't understand the definition of an insult. After all, you've been hurling insults around for so long you probably don't even notice them anymore. Sort of the same principle behind all that perfume you wear."

"I see," I hissed out. "Maybe you can clarify things for me then. For example, if I were to tell you . . . say, to drop dead, would that be an insult or simply an instruction?"

"See, you can't even go three seconds without starting up again."

"I didn't lose."

He held up one hand in protest and then let it drop back onto his lap. "All right. I'm willing to let this infraction slide, but you have to start all over again. You have to go a full week from today without insulting another person."

"I'll go two weeks," I said, just because I hated his patronizing tone.

"Fine. Two weeks."

I immediately regretted I'd volunteered for an extra week, but I didn't try to take it back.

"Let's set some rules," he went on, "just so you and I agree on the definition of an insult. If it isn't kind, and it isn't something you'd want someone saying about you, then it's an insult, and you lose our bet. Agreed?"

I wanted to tell him what he could do with his rules and his stupid bet, but he would never let me live it down if I did. He'd still be calling me a cheater and a weasel at our ten-year reunion. My pride was riding on this bet now. "Agreed."

"So, where do you want Doug to take you on your date?"

He was fishing for insults, but I wasn't about to be taken in so easily. "As long as you're sitting here, why don't you help me with these posters. After all, you'll be working on my campaign soon enough anyway."

"I can't. I've got tons of homework to do." He picked up his backpack and stood up. I watched him go, and when he was almost out of earshot, I said, "Reverse psychology is a wonderful thing." It wasn't really an insult. Not technically anyway.

As I suspected, Logan hadn't been gone thirty seconds before my friends started in. "What was that all about?" Aubrie asked.

I pressed another star onto my poster. "Just some stupid bet we have going. He thinks I can't go two weeks without insulting someone."

"And you took the bet?" Chelsea asked—which just goes to prove what she really thinks of me.

"Yes, I took the bet. I can do it."

Aubrie and Chelsea looked at each other, then both started laughing. I chucked one of the stars at them.

"I can do it," I said again.

Aubrie pursed her lips together in a teasing smile. "I think he was flirting with you."

"When? When he called me a cheater, or when he told me I wear too much perfume?"

"No," Aubrie said slowly. "It was the way he looked at you."

"Doubtful. He just wants me to go out with Doug so Doug will set him up with some chick named Veronica."

"That's probably a front," she said.

I nearly called her crazy, but figured that might classify as an insult.

At this point, Rachel traipsed back over to us. "I got six more signatures just to make sure we have enough." She dropped the papers by me, then sat down and stretched out her legs. "Did I miss anything while I was gone?"

Aubrie winked over at her. "Just Logan Hansen hitting on Samantha."

"He wasn't hitting on me. He was trying to make my life difficult."

Chelsea smiled and tossed Rachel a marker. "Some guys don't differentiate between the two."

"Oh!" Rachel held up one hand, as though just remembering. "Amy and her friends are upstairs making campaign posters. It looks like vandalism on poster board. I mean, they're just writing stupid stuff."

She turned to me for some commentary, and I tried to think of something that wouldn't be unkind nor would I mind if someone said it about me. Rachel waited, her puzzlement growing with my silence. Finally Chelsea said, "Don't mind Samantha. She's on an insult-free diet."

I rolled my eyes at Chelsea because Logan hadn't said anything about facial expressions in his rules.

Aubrie looked over at Rachel and told her, "Logan bet

Samantha she couldn't go two weeks without insulting anyone."

"Oh," Rachel said in a sad sort of way. "I hope you don't have a lot riding on it."

I put the last star on my poster, pressing it down so hard that glue squeezed out underneath the edges. "Your faith in me is so touching."

It was really beginning to bug me that no one thought I could win this bet. After all, it wasn't like I insulted people all of the time. I didn't. Well, at least I didn't insult people any more than everybody else insulted people. "Back to the issue of posters," I said. "How many do you think we should make?"

"I think we should make a ton of posters and take all of the good hall spaces," Aubrie said.

"I think we should wait to see where Amy puts her posters and then put ours next to hers," Chelsea said. "That way everyone will be able to make the comparison between good and trashy."

"Let's just take Amy's posters down when we see them," Rachel added. "We'll call it introducing Amy to the constituents in the garbage can."

I slid my poster over to Chelsea so she could do the lettering. "That wouldn't be fair."

"Samantha's right. That wouldn't be fair," said Aubrie.

Chelsea shrugged. "You know what they say: All's fair in love, war, and high school."

"We'd get in trouble if we got caught. I'd probably be kicked out of the race."

"So you won't take them down," Rachel said, "and we won't get caught doing it. It'll be easy."

I hated to tell them no. After all, they were my friends, and they were trying to help me. They had just taken time out of their schedules to make posters for me. Still, I knew ripping the other candidates' posters down wasn't right. "I don't want to run a mean campaign. I don't think I have to. I can beat Amy and Rick on merit alone."

My friends exchanged glances, but didn't offer opinions otherwise. "Okay," Chelsea said. "We'll be nice. At least for now."

All in all we made six posters, which was good for our first day. And they looked crisp and professional. Mine would be the nicest posters. Rachel had already said Amy's were lousy, and Rick wouldn't come up with anything good. Rick probably didn't even know how to spell two of the three words in the sentence "Vote for Rick."

We hung up the posters around the school hallways, and then I told everyone I'd clean up the art supplies so they could go home. I felt bad making them stay any later on my account.

I stuffed what I could into my backpack, stacked up what I needed to carry, and then picked up all the scraps of paper to throw away. Cassidy walked by as I was hauling stuff to the garbage can. She stopped when she saw me.

"Hi, Samantha."

"Hi." I dropped the last of the scraps into the garbage can and tried to brush off some dried glue stuck on one hand.

"I saw some of your posters. They look really good."

"Thanks. Were you here helping Amy with hers?"

"Yeah, but our posters aren't nearly as nice as yours. You ought to be glad I didn't help you after all."

If she hadn't said this, I probably never would have brought up the subject, but somehow seeing her standing in front of me smiling and chatting, like she was really my friend, just irritated me to death.

"You know, Cassidy, I still remember last year when you wrote me that note. The one that said you were sorry we'd been fighting and you hoped we could be friends. I guess you didn't really mean any of those things, did you?"

She blinked at me with a stunned expression. "Yes, I meant it."

"Then how come you're campaigning for my opponent?"

"Because Amy is my friend too. Besides, she needs my help more than you do. You have lots of friends to help you."

I held one glue-covered hand out to Cassidy pleadingly. "I need your help more than anybody. I really, really need to win this election. I mean, what does it matter to Amy whether she wins or not? She has the grades to go anywhere."

"The grades to go anywhere?" Cassidy repeated.

At first I didn't say anything. I just stood there by the garbage can wavering between reason and hope. It seemed like a dangerous thing to do—to give your opponent information about yourself that could be used against you—but when it came right down to it, I trusted Cassidy. If she understood what was really at stake, if I gave her a good enough reason, she'd leave Amy's campaign and help me.

"You've always planned on going to a good college, haven't you?" I asked.

"I guess."

"Well, so have I, but my grades are only average, and I bombed the SATs."

She shifted her backpack from one shoulder to the other. "You still have next year to bring your score up."

"I'm going to, but this year I got an eight ten. I need to be president to boost my chances of being accepted someplace I'd actually want to go."

Cassidy opened her mouth in protest, but I went on before she could. "I know it sounds calculated, but in the long run it's not going to matter to Amy whether she wins or not. For me, this election could decide my future."

For a moment there was silence between us. I'd put forth my argument on one end of the scale, and I waited for her to put her decision on the other.

With a shrug of her shoulders she delivered her verdict. "I'd like to help you, but I'm not sure running for president is the answer to your college application problems. I mean, shouldn't you run for president because you actually want to be president?"

"I do want to be president," I said. "Weren't you just listening to what I said?"

"No, I mean, Amy is running because she'd like to go into politics one day. She has some good ideas about running the school and doing community projects. She's really organized and stuff."

I couldn't believe it. I had opened my soul to Cassidy, and in return she handed me an Amy campaign speech.

I said, "Thanks a lot, Cassidy. I can tell how badly you want to be my friend," then turned and walked away from her.

When I got home from school, I dropped my backpack on the countertop and opened the fridge. A pan full of something that looked like burned pears in gravy lay on the top shelf.

Mom sat at the kitchen table helping Andy with his homework. She called over to me, "The crème de poire is for dessert tonight. Don't get into it now."

As if that were a temptation.

Why couldn't my mother have been one of those types that baked cookies? When you wanted to drown your sorrows in something, crème de poire didn't come to mind. I pushed aside the pan in an attempt to find something edible. Condiments, soy sauce, pickled anchovies. I didn't even want to ask what she planned on doing with those. I grabbed an apple from the crisper and shut the fridge.

"Did anybody call for me?" I hoped, I really did, that a guy had called, and I would have a reason to break free of my lousy mood.

Without looking up from Andy's homework, she said, "Nope. Who are you expecting?"

"Nobody. I guess I'm not expecting anybody to call me."

Mom turned in her chair to face me. "You and Brad haven't made up yet?"

"No. And pigs still don't fly, either."

Mom mumbled something to Andy about his paper, then stood and walked closer to me. "I'm sorry Samantha, but you'll find someone to take his place."

"I don't know. It's so hard to find men these days who appreciate feline head-ware."

She let out a sigh. "You're never going to let that cat incident drop, are you?"

I took a bite of my apple.

Mom took a dishcloth from the sink and wiped off the

counter beside me. "If you try too hard to get a guy's attention, it just scares him away. Don't worry about it, and things will start to look up."

Mom loved to give me dating advice. She hadn't been on a real date in twenty years, but she still considered herself an expert on all matters pertaining to relationships. Usually I only half listened to what she said, but today I wanted her to reassure me everything would work out all right. I wanted her to promise me I wouldn't sit home on prom night and have nothing to do but drown my sorrows in strange French cuisine.

"Prom is two weeks from tomorrow," I told her quietly.

"So why don't you ask someone?"

"You don't do that for the prom," I said, but suddenly I wasn't so sure. After all, some girls did do the asking if their boyfriend lived in another city, or was an underclassman, or had already graduated.

I took my apple upstairs and thought about a guy who'd graduated—a guy with dark hair and deep blue eyes who was coming back to Pullman any day now to work in his parents' store.

Josh lingered in my thoughts all weekend. By Monday morning I not only wanted to go to the prom with him, I wanted to honeymoon in Spain with him. The thing about Josh was, he was not only gorgeous, he was gentlemanly. The kind of guy who opened doors for women and was polite to his mother. Last year while I cheered at the football games, I saw him more than once giving his little sister a piggyback ride to the concession stand. How sweet is that? Josh would never leave his date stranded in a parking lot. And even his name had a romantic quality to it. You could passionately whisper "Josh" over and over again without getting tongue-tied.

I was in such a good mood about this prom possibility, I didn't even get steamed when I walked to my locker and noticed that one of my posters was engulfed by a row of vote-for-Rick posters. They all said the same thing: Rick Rocks. Apparently he was going for quantity, and not quality. Either that or his spelling was even more limited than I'd supposed. It didn't matter. I still had plenty of time to make more posters, and mine would all be unique.

After I put my things away, I went and found my friends standing in our spot by the cafeteria. Chelsea was doing her usual nitpicking about peoples' outfits, but just to keep myself in good mental condition, I kept my commentaries upbeat. After each one of Chelsea's critiques, I said, "But I'm sure she's a very nice person anyway."

Finally Chelsea turned to me and said, "Samantha, stop it."

"Stop what?"

Her face tilted down in a patronizing manner. "I wasn't judging peoples' personalities, just their ability to keep basic fashion rules."

"I have to think positively, or I'll slip up and lose my bet."

Rachel rolled her eyes and gave a small snort. "You know, there are worse things than going out with Doug Campton."

"Like what?"

"Like driving us all crazy with your Little Miss Sunshine routine."

Aubrie nodded. "If you were any perkier, PBS would drag you away and put you on 'Barney and Friends.' "

"They would not." Which just goes to show that you can't please everyone. Last week Logan insisted I could enter an Olympic event in snideness, and now my friends were accusing me of being able to host my own children's show.

Chelsea elbowed me. "There goes Amy, and she looks like she's dressed to kill—or at least like she killed one of the seven dwarfs to get that outfit. Go ahead and insult her. You'll feel better afterward."

I shook my head. "I'm not going to do it."

"Oh, come on," Rachel said. "It's not like we'll tell Logan. You can trust us."

"No way," I said. "You're the one who said I should go out with Doug. You obviously don't have my best interests at heart."

Chelsea humphed. "All right. If you want to continue

with this syrupy sweet escapade, that's fine. Just tone it down while you're around us."

As if being complimentary was some sort of character flaw.

Despite what my friends thought, I had to win this bet. I couldn't admit that I couldn't go two weeks without insulting someone—not to myself, and certainly not to Logan. Watching him gloat about it would be worse than going out with Doug.

Far worse.

My friends just didn't understand about Logan. They'd come to rely on my scathing commentaries on high-school social life as part of their daily routine. Everything would be back to normal after my two weeks were up. Until then I just had to throw in my lot with Barney the dinosaur.

I actually repeated the words *compliments, compliments, compliments* to myself as I walked through the hallways in between classes. I had to do this because I was afraid Logan actually had told people to spy on me, and I wasn't sure who might report my doings back to him.

Today Logan caught up with me as I went to lunch. He walked along beside me with a smile. "So how's your day going?"

"Great. Couldn't be better." I picked up my pace, but Logan kept alongside.

"Did Mr. Peterson give you the lecture on Freud in sociology?"

"Yep. Mr. Peterson is, as always, a wonderful lecturer."

"So, do you think all women really have a deep-seated desire to be men?"

Only in Freud's crazed and demented world. "Probably not," I said.

"Then why do you think Freud came up with the theory?"

I could see the cafeteria. It was only steps away. Still, I couldn't resist answering Logan's question. "Freud obviously hung around too many men."

"Is that an insult?"

"Only if you consider the term *men* to be insulting."

He looked at me suspiciously, but I reached the table where my friends sat and pulled out a chair for myself. I waved good-bye to Logan with a smile and called out, "Have a great lunch!"

He walked past the table, shaking his head.

"Have a great lunch?" Rachel asked. She rolled her eyes.

I got my own sandwich out of my bag and glared back at her. "You could at least try to be a little bit supportive of my dilemma. Being nice isn't as easy as it looks, you know."

We all ate silently for a few minutes, and might have done so indefinitely if Rick hadn't stopped by our table. He sauntered up to us wearing a T-shirt that read ANARCHY NOW and grinned benevolently down at us. "Hi, girls."

"Hi, Rick," I said, because I knew he was really talking to me.

He ran one hand across his spiky, supposed-to-be-dyed-blond-but-actually-looked-more-like-florescent-yellow hair. "I'm throwing a pre-victory party at my house on Friday. You're all invited, of course, because I'm a good sport."

A hundred things I could say ran through my mind, but I didn't utter any of them. For all I knew, Logan had set this up. I said, "Uh, thanks, Rick, but I don't think we'll make it."

"Too bad," Rick said. "A lot of your friends will be there."

Chelsea shook her head. "Stop being such a moron and go away."

Rick put his hand to his chest, as though wounded. "Hey, don't get me wrong. If I could have chosen an opponent, I would have chosen you, Samantha. In fact, I have a good motto for you." He then waved his hand as if he were placing each word on an invisible poster. "SAMANTHA TAYLOR. SHE PUTS THE CAN-I-DATE IN CANDIDATE."

"Thanks for the help," I said stiffly. "But why don't you stick to your own campaign." And maybe you could come up with a slogan that doesn't involve rocks.

"Oh, I'm more than happy to help you," he said. "Because I think cheerleaders can use all the help they can get. How about this: SAMANTHA. SHE'S THE SIS WITH THE BOOM BAH."

I smiled back at him. "How about: Rick—" I almost added, *He puts the pain in campaign,* but I stopped myself just in time. Then I stared up at him, searching for something that would make sense and wouldn't be an insult. I couldn't think of anything.

Rick waited for me to finish my sentence for another moment, but when I didn't, he said, "How about Rick. Now that's catchy, Samantha. You ought to go into advertising." He laughed at his own joke and turned away.

Chelsea shook her head at me. "You sure told him where to get off."

Aubrie reached over and patted my hand. "I'll say it for you. How about: Rick, he's an ultimate, supreme, pathetic jerk."

"That was good," Rachel said, "but lacking the Samantha signature umph."

I picked up a potato chip from my lunch and bit into it viciously. "All I'm going to say on the subject is this: I'm going to enjoy defeating Rick. The umph will have to come later."

During my English class I thought about the campaign speech I had to deliver to the student body before the elections. I'd stress the need to elect someone responsible. I'd emphasize the fact that school events were not parties, and the student body needed someone without rocks in their brains to be in charge of them.

But not only did this speech start to sound silly, I began to wonder if it would actually work against me. If I emphasized responsibility, people would start thinking of Amy, wouldn't they? She was one of those students who always had her homework neatly organized in her folder and was never late for anything.

I needed to emphasize things I was good at, like school spirit and . . . um . . . the ability to represent my school in a good manner. I mean, the student body ought to be embarrassed to elect someone who stuck safety pins through his ears.

I thought about this for a while, but couldn't come up with a way of putting it into a speech that sounded good. Somehow, you just didn't say, "If elected, I promise to work hard, promote unity, and never put sewing equipment through parts of my body."

So after a while I just thought of all of the things I'd say to Rick after he lost the election. In my fantasies I was condescending and aloof. The only problem was, no matter what I said to Rick, his reply was always the same. He shrugged and said, "I don't care that I lost. It was all just a big joke anyway."

And that really summed up the situation with Rick. He

didn't care. Everyone knew he didn't care, and I shouldn't waste my time worrying about him. Chances were he'd get tired of this whole charade before elections and drop out of the race, or be suspended from school, or, at the very least, give a really stupid campaign speech in which he promised to sell whiskey in the cafeteria and fire the teachers.

Rick wasn't my problem. Amy was. She was my only real contender in this race, and both she and I knew it. I couldn't afford to forget this again.

After English, I headed toward my next class. I had just walked up the stairs when Doug appeared at my side. He clutched a couple of books in one hand while simultaneously swinging his arms in a way that made me wonder if his books would, at any moment, go flying into the air. "Hey," he said to me. "What's a girl like you doing in a place like this?"

"At the moment, biology." I didn't slow my pace.

"Ahh, biology. I have that first period." He nodded his head knowingly. "There's just nothing like learning about the caribou mating habits to get your day started." And then, right there in the hallway, Doug let forth this sound from his throat that sounded halfway between a yodel and a gorilla being strangled.

Everyone in the vicinity turned to stare at us. I walked more quickly, grasping my books against my chest as though Doug might have just been overcome with insanity and any moment now he would either pounce on me or climb up the lockers and try to fly.

He grinned, oblivious to all the hallway attention still focused on us. "That was my caribou mating call."

Oh. How romantic. Exactly how did he want me to respond to that? Was I supposed to yodel back or shoot him?

I kept walking quickly. "What class do you have now?" *And shouldn't you be going there instead of trying to attract caribou?*

"Math."

Dang. It was in the same direction as biology. That meant I had several more minutes of conversation time with Doug. Time in which he could put on other hallway performances. Time in which he could ask me anything.

Did he know I didn't have a date to the prom?

Think. Think. Think. I needed to say something, anything that wouldn't give him the opportunity to lead the conversation in that direction.

"Math," I said cheerily, "math is a good class. You can't get enough of math."

He let out a grunt. "I can." And he trained his gaze on my eyes. "I can think of a million other things I'd rather do."

Oops, that sentence could lead anywhere—like to us standing together in front of the prom photographer.

"Well, of course math isn't the funnest thing. Really, when you come right down to it, English would have to be my favorite class. Mrs. Mortenson is such a good teacher. I mean, she knows all about theme, plot, symbolism—who knew books were so involved?"

As long as the topic stayed on school, I was safe, and I was prepared to talk about school nonstop, without breathing if necessary, for the rest of the walk to my class.

"You would think you'd get enough of books at your job."

"My job?" He knew about my job? What else did he know about me?

"Logan said you work at The Bookie with him, right?"

"Right."

Logan told him about me. How nice. I would have to thank Logan for this the next time I saw him.

Doug glanced blankly around at the lockers as we walked. "It must be a boring job. Sort of like working at the library. You have to be quiet all of the time." Now his gaze turned back to me. "I bet you can't wait until your shift is over, and you can cut loose and have fun."

And there we were again, heading away from school topics and going places where you wore corsages.

"I like my job most of the time. It has its problems, but then all jobs do. And of course, working with Logan is the biggest—" I stopped myself before I added the word *problem.* I couldn't let any insults creep out of my mouth and find their way back to Logan. Instead, I smiled as though I was simply trying to find the right adjective and said, "pleasure."

Doug cocked his head. "Working with Logan is a pleasure?"

"No one stacks and shelves the way he does. It's one of his best talents." With the same smile still plastered on my face, I added, "You'll have to ask him to arrange your locker for you sometime. Really. He'd love to do it for you."

Doug raised an eyebrow, but before he could comment about Logan's organizational skills, or anything else, I saw my chance for escape. The girls' bathroom was off to my left.

I veered sharply in that direction and gave Doug a wave as I did. "See you later."

Once inside the bathroom, I leaned up against the wall and stared at myself in the mirror. I didn't want to have to keep worrying about this type of thing. I didn't want to have to dart through the hallways avoiding Doug. I needed a date for the prom. Soon.

I couldn't think about anything else for the rest of the day, which is why, when school ended and I headed down the school steps, I almost thought I was imagining things. There, standing on the school steps, looking like the angel-of-teenage-girls'-daydreams had just dropped him off, was Josh.

I nearly stumbled at the sight of him. I caught myself before I did—which was a good thing, since I'm sure the very last way to impress a guy is to pitch yourself down a flight of stairs, arms waving and books flying in all directions. Josh was turned sideways talking to someone, so he didn't see my hesitancy. Another good thing. I had a moment to compose myself before I walked up to him.

And I was going to walk up to him. I was going to walk up and say something charming and witty. I wasn't sure what, but I had a dozen steps to figure it out.

One.

Two.

Three.

Four.

Okay, I couldn't come up with anything charming or witty, but I was still going to stop, say hi, and welcome him back to Pullman.

Then I saw who Josh was talking to—Logan. I was half tempted to keep on walking, but instead I called out, "Hey Josh, what brings you back to high school?"

He glanced up and gave me a grin that nearly toppled me down the rest of the stairs anyway. "I'm meeting Elise here to give her a ride to our store. She's helping me do inventory today."

Great. If I stayed here talking to Josh, I'd have to endure not only Logan but also Elise.

Still, I smiled back at Josh and stayed. That's how good he looked.

Logan ignored me and continued the conversation he'd been having with Josh. "So who else did you see from Pullman at college?"

"Bob and I had chemistry together, and I wouldn't have survived it without his help. He aced all his classes. He was one of the few freshmen I knew who actually had time for socializing."

I leaned a bit closer to Josh. "Somehow I can't imagine you sat home every night."

"No, of course not," he said. "I spent every night at the library."

I laughed lightly, and Logan raised an eyebrow at me. He was wondering why I was here, and I was wishing he would leave. I wanted him to go away so Josh could look at me softly and tell me he'd been a fool last year not to sweep me off my feet. Both of us stayed put. I ignored Logan and watched Josh talk, watched the way his blue eyes reflected the sunlight like they were two pieces of the sky.

Not only would we honeymoon in Spain, we'd buy a small villa there and spend our evenings listening to castanet music and dancing underneath the stars.

Logan said, "But then you've always hated biology class, haven't you, Samantha?"

I had no idea what the conversation currently was about, and I struggled to think of a reply that wouldn't expose this. "I have other classes I like more."

Logan snapped his fingers. "What was that limerick you

made up about Mr. Jones? Something about him being a missing link?"

Actually the limerick said Mr. Jones was missing all of his links, but I didn't correct Logan. "That was so long ago. I really don't remember." Then with a smile I added, "Mr. Jones is really a very good teacher and a nice man."

Josh nodded. "Sometimes the harder they are, the more you learn."

"Uh-huh." Logan's eyes narrowed. "And what about that lab partner you got stuck with last semester. Remember when he set your biology book on fire? What was that name you always called him at work?"

"Adam," I said. "His name was Adam."

"Uh-huh," Logan said again.

I smiled over at Josh. "So are you glad to be home?"

He turned his sky-blue eyes on me. "Sure, and getting gladder all the time."

Was he flirting or just glad to be out of biology class? I leaned even closer to him. "Maybe now you'll be able to catch up on your social life."

"More likely, I'll get my dad caught up on every backyard-landscaping project he's had since last September."

Did Josh not get my hint, or was he just choosing to ignore it?

Logan, however, understood. He looked at me and then rolled his eyes like he couldn't believe I was hitting on Josh on the school steps.

Josh didn't notice the exchange between Logan and me. He lifted a hand and waved to someone up the stairs, then called out, "Elise, over here."

Not only Elise but Cassidy walked down to where we stood. And Cassidy shot me a sharp glare.

Cassidy, who always wore a saintly expression of kindness, looked like she wanted to burn down my villa in Spain.

So, it wasn't as over for her as she'd professed.

Elise said, "Josh, what are you doing here?" and then added, "Oh, that's right. I forgot you were coming to pick me up."

Elise would have failed a drama class. She couldn't even pull off acting surprised. She had obviously not told Cassidy that Josh was coming to the school, and she was feigning forgetfulness as an excuse for putting her friend in an uncomfortable situation. She smiled over at Cassidy and added, "Do you want us to drop you off at your house? It'll be just like old times."

Cassidy held her books closer against her chest. "No, that's all right. It's out of your way."

"It's no problem," Josh said.

"No, really," Cassidy said. "See you guys tomorrow." Then she walked down the rest of the steps.

Josh watched her go, and I watched Josh watch her go. Logan must have watched me watching Josh watch her, because when I turned back to the group, Logan rolled his eyes at me again.

Josh reached into his pocket and took out his car keys. "Well, I guess we'd better not keep Dad waiting."

Elise just sighed and said, "Okay, let's go."

As they went down the rest of the stairs Josh turned and said, "Nice seeing you guys again," but he looked at me as he said it, and he smiled. Which was a good sign, wasn't it?

I stood on the stairs, not wanting to follow right after him—that would be awkward since he'd just said good-bye to me—and yet not really having any reason to stay on the stairs.

Logan folded his arms and shook his head slowly at me. "So tell me, do you just naturally flirt with every guy in the vicinity? Is it some sort of compulsion that you can't help?"

"I don't flirt with you."

"Then you're saying you think about it beforehand. You lay out your web like a spider waiting for its prey."

I bit my lip before I could tell him what species in the animal kingdom he was most like.

Compliments . . . compliments . . . one quick shove and he'll go flying down the stairs . . .

I marshaled all my self-control. "How come I can't insult you, but you have no qualms about insulting me?"

"Well, I guess that's because we didn't make a bet that *I* couldn't go two weeks without insulting people." He smiled, showing a set of perfectly white teeth. "You still have ten days left." He started down the steps himself. "You know, it's gonna be a fun ten days."

I thought about Josh off and on at school the next day. I especially thought about him in between classes while I was avoiding Doug in the hallways.

I would have preferred to run into Josh here and there around town and wait for something to happen between us. That's how romances ideally develop, but the prom was coming up. I needed to be bold.

Only I wasn't quite sure how to go about being bold. Did I call him to chat, and then see how he acted? Ask him outright? Maybe drop by the office-supply store Josh worked at and casually buy thousands of Post-it notes while I worked up my courage? What did one say to a guy who had rejected you the year before?

The confident approach: "So, are you any smarter about women this year?"

The witty approach: "So, I see you've changed a lot of things about yourself. Did you change your mind too?"

Or perhaps I could just go with the desperate approach: "Please tell me I'm not second-best anymore."

When the last bell rang, I followed the throng of students out the door, still contemplating it all. I never made it to the parking lot. Rachel and Aubrie intercepted me halfway down the school steps.

"There you are," Aubrie said.

"We have to talk." Rachel looked around as if trying to assess the best place. "Let's go back inside."

"What is it?"

Neither of them answered until we went back up the school steps and stood by the gym, away from the main flow of students. Then Rachel unfolded a piece of yellow paper for me to see. "Someone put flyers on all the car windshields."

In large handwriting it said:

Vote for Samantha Taylor?
She got an 810 on the S.A.T.
Be smart and vote for someone else.

As soon as I read it, I swear, my stomach jumped up and grabbed on to my throat. I didn't know what to say. I just stood there gripping the flyer and repeated "Oh, no!" about seventeen times.

Before I made it to the eighteenth, Rachel said, "Who did you tell about your SAT score?"

It wasn't hard to pick the culprit. "Cassidy Woodruff."

Rachel put her hands on her hips and cocked her head at me. "And why would you have been stupid enough to do that?"

"I trusted her. I thought I could convince her to come over to our side."

"How? By letting her know you're an idiot?"

I crumpled up the flyer, trying to smash the words off the paper. "You don't need to rub it in."

I stepped over to a hall trash can and shoved the flyer inside. As I did, Rachel took my arm and tried to stop me. "Hey, wait, we need that as evidence."

It was too late, though. I'd already put the flyer in the trash, and I was not about to put my hand in there to try and find it.

"Don't worry," Aubrie said glumly. "There are tons more of them outside."

I groaned. My stomach had not only grabbed on to my throat, it was now trying to climb up. Aubrie and Rachel walked back outside, and I followed after them. We spent the next few minutes taking the flyers off the cars that were still in the parking lot. Which wasn't many. Most of the students at PHS didn't stick around long after the bell rang.

Ripping flyers off windshields was a totally humiliating experience. Each time I saw my name on those papers, it caused a jabbing feeling in the place my stomach used to be. How many students saw this flyer? And what would they think of me now? Would I be remembered not as a leader, but just as some stupid cheerleader? I wished I had never run for president. I wished the next time Cassidy gave someone that phony smile, her face broke in half.

After we finished with the windshields, we started on the rest of the parking lot. Flyers lay scattered from one end to the other. I assumed most people just pulled them off their windshields and left them on the ground—which, in a way, was a good sign for me. At least it meant no one took them home to keep as treasured mementos. Maybe some of the kids didn't even read them. Maybe it wouldn't be a big deal at all.

I clutched the stack of flyers in my hand. Who was I kidding? This was war, and I'd just been dealt an ugly, ugly blow.

Only I wasn't about to declare this battle over. Oh, no. I'd just begun to fight. I regretted I only had but one life to give to my cause . . . and whatever that other war saying was . . . something about torpedoes. Anyway, if Amy wanted a fight, I'd give it to her.

After we'd collected all of the flyers, we sat down on a grassy hill by the parking lot to plan our counterattack.

"I say we take these flyers into the office and have Amy busted," I said.

Aubrie shook her head. "They won't do anything about it. We can't prove she was the one who did it."

"They could match her handwriting."

Rachel grunted. "That's not Amy's handwriting. She wouldn't have been foolish enough to write them herself." She held up one of the flyers until it was just inches away from her face. "Besides, it's a guy's handwriting."

Now I examined one of the papers. It did look like a guy's writing. The lettering didn't flow. It just stuck up in tall, uneven lines—like whoever wrote it was in a hurry. Guys' writing always looks that way.

So Amy must have had a friend, or a brother, or some lowlife from her criminal double existence write it for her. Someone untraceable. Still, I studied every single letter on the flyer in hopes I'd be able to recognize it if I ever saw it again.

Most of it could have been anybody's writing, but the *e*'s were distinctive. Their loops pointed up in skinny juts, almost like they were sloppy *i*'s. I'd watch for those *e*'s again, probably for the rest of my life. Someday I'd be in a nursing home and notice that the old man sitting next to me wrote those kinds of *e*'s. Then I'd reach over and smack him with my cane.

Rachel nodded toward the school. "I say we rip down all of Amy's posters."

I thought about it for a moment, but only for a moment. Those speeches on fairness and how I didn't want to run a mean campaign seemed very far away, their words faint. Much fainter than the handwriting in front of me. "Yeah," I said softly. "That would make me feel better."

We left the parking lot and walked back to the school. A few people still straggled down the stairs. How many students and, more importantly, how many teachers were inside?

If my stomach hadn't already gone AWOL, it would have fled now. I wished Chelsea was here with us. Chelsea wasn't afraid of anything, and I could have used some of her courage. But she walked home every day and must not have seen the flyers. I envied her ignorance.

I whispered to the others, "We're just getting stuff from our lockers. Act casual."

Rachel rolled her eyes at me. "You think? I'd planned on darting suspiciously back and forth down the hallways."

I walked faster. I didn't need her sarcasm. I wanted to tell her to forget the whole thing. I'd take care of the posters myself. But the truth was, I needed my friends' help. I couldn't risk getting caught taking the posters down myself.

We walked into a hallway that had two Amy posters hanging on the walls. "All right," I said. "I'll stand guard and make sure the coast is clear. If anyone comes this way, I'll start coughing."

"What if someone comes from the other end of the hallway?" Aubrie asked.

"No one will," Rachel said, and pulled Aubrie toward the posters. I could tell Rachel just wanted to get the whole thing over with. Maybe she wanted it over so badly she wouldn't be careful. After all, it wasn't her presidency at stake. I hoped she'd at least look around before she started ripping things down.

I glanced at them as they walked toward a poster, then turned the other way. It wouldn't do any good to have me stand guard if I didn't pay attention.

The hallway in front of me stood silent and empty, but what if someone came? Would Rachel and Aubrie even hear my coughing? Maybe if I also pretended to have a seizure at the same time, it would cause such a commotion that no one would notice Rachel and Aubrie shoving large pieces of poster board into the garbage can.

I scanned the hallway in front of me for a minute and listened to the quiet in the hallway behind me. Were they finished? It seemed like they should be, but I didn't want to turn around in case I missed someone approaching.

I waited.

And waited.

When I was just about to turn around and check on my friends, a guy from my Spanish class turned the corner and walked down the hall toward me.

I didn't know much about Bentley Roberts beyond the fact that he spoke Spanish well and was really annoying about it. He'd spent the last summer in South America in a student exchange program and now considered himself an expert on all things Latino. Occasionally he corrected us on our accents in class or told us our *d*'s weren't soft enough. I avoided him when I could. Now he walked right toward me.

I coughed, and then coughed again. I still didn't hear anything from behind me, so I coughed louder, this time thumping my chest for added effect.

Bentley paused as he came to me. "Are you all right?"

"Yeah—" I coughed again. "I just have"—I added a few more coughs—"—allergies."

His brows furrowed, as though he expected me to collapse at any moment. "Are you going to be okay?"

I would be if Rachel and Aubrie suddenly appeared. What were they waiting for—the paramedics? "Oh sure—" cough, cough. "It comes and goes." I patted my chest as though the coughing were about to subside.

Bentley nodded, but didn't go past me. He still wore a look of concern. "What are you allergic to?"

"Um," this was an answer I should have known, but didn't. I struggled for a moment to think of something—anything—people were allergic to. "Ragweed," I said, and then because he seemed to be looking around the hallway in search of a ragweed bush, I added, "Sometimes I just get an attack out of the blue."

"Oh."

I tried to think of something else to stall him. "Don't you have any allergies?"

"No, but whenever I drink milk, I get indigestion."

"Oh. Well. Sorry to hear that." I could think of absolutely nothing else to say to that, so I just stood there staring at him for a moment. When he was about to walk past me, I blurted out, "That must be hard. I mean, how do you eat cold cereal in the morning?"

"Usually I don't. I just have toast."

I nodded as though I found this a fascinating fact. "I guess

I'm lucky ragweed doesn't belong to one of the four food groups."

"They make non-dairy milk you can put on cereal, but it doesn't taste the same."

"Oh." And that was about as far as I could drag this conversation out.

"Well, I hope you feel better," he said, and walked past me.

I turned around and looked down the hallway. Except for Bentley, it was empty.

They weren't even there? I had been talking indigestion with Bentley for nothing? I stared down the hallway and wondered what to do next.

Could my friends have been caught by someone coming up the other end of the hallway? Perhaps right now the principal was chewing them out in her office.

I walked down the hallway and peered into the next one. It was empty too. I tapped my foot nervously, looking around the rows of lockers. Seconds, minutes, millennia went by. I walked back to the first hallway. And that's where I found Aubrie and Rachel. They walked casually toward me, as though strolling around the school hallways after school was a normal activity.

When they got close to me, I whispered, "Where have you been?"

"Taking down posters," Rachel whispered back. "We finished in this hallway and just figured it would be faster to move on to the next one without coming back to get you."

I hadn't realized I was shaking, but I suddenly felt it and wrapped my arms around my waist. "Thanks a lot. I've been back here coughing my lungs up."

"Well, you can be happy now. It's done, and we didn't get caught."

"Yet," Aubrie said.

Rachel and I both got her point. We quickly walked toward the front door.

I didn't breathe easily again until we reached the parking lot. And then I took several deep breaths. It was done. It didn't seem like nearly enough payback considering how Amy had smeared my name, but at least now she'd think twice before doing any more dirty campaigning.

Aubrie took her car keys out of her backpack. "Now we can all go home and relax."

"Yeah," I said, and suddenly realized I couldn't. I was supposed to be at work at 3:45. I looked at my watch. It read 3:42. Not only would I not have time to go to Josh's store, I wouldn't have time to go home and grab anything to eat, either. Usually I ate a sandwich or something because I worked through the dinner hour. Today I'd have to settle for whatever was on the candy rack by the registers. After all of the tension of the day, this was just what my stomach needed—a meal that consisted of Blowcharms and Trident.

I said good-bye to my friends, threw my backpack into my car, and drove out of the parking lot like I was Brad with half a dozen cats roaming around the front seat.

When I walked into the bookstore, I saw Logan standing at the cart. He always drove to school, which meant he'd been one of the lucky recipients of a flyer with my SAT score on it. He was probably just bursting with happiness and would gloat about my lousy score for the entire shift.

I should have just gone home and called in sick.

I walked over to the closet and got my vest out. Logan strolled up beside me as I put it on. "Hi."

"Just shut up," I told him.

"What?" He raised his eyebrows in surprise. "What did I say?"

I buttoned up the vest and wished my fingers would stop shaking. "It's not what you said, it's what you're about to say."

"You know what I'm going to say? Now you're a psychic?"

"No. I'm obviously not a psychic. A psychic would have done really well on say . . . the SAT."

"Oh," he nodded in an unconcerned manner. "So the report was true?"

"I was having a bad day when I took the test," I lied. "I had this huge headache, and I couldn't think straight."

Logan shrugged. "You'll do better when you retake them."

"Yeah, I will."

I waited for him to say something else to me, some jibe or jest, some commentary on my intelligence. But he didn't. He just went back to the book cart. I waited a little longer. Why in the world was he being nice to me now—now when he had really great ammunition to use against me? I decided not to live with the suspense.

I went over to the cart, and while I picked up books, I said, "Aren't you going to tell me some dumb-blond jokes or something?"

He glanced over at me with a smile. "Naw, I figure you've heard them all before."

That was more like the Logan I knew.

"I suppose you aced your test," I said.

"If I didn't, I'm smart enough not to have told everyone about it."

I slipped another book underneath my arm. "I didn't tell everyone. I just told Cassidy Woodruff. I didn't think she was the vindictive type." I paused for a moment, then added, "You notice I didn't tell you."

He leaned over the book cart toward me and smiled again. "Was that an insult?"

"No. It was a veiled suggestion. It's not my fault you're smart enough to figure it out."

I thought he'd fight this point, but instead, he straightened up and tapped a book absentmindedly against the cart. "Cassidy Woodruff. Why would she put flyers about you on people's windshields?"

"She's campaigning for Amy."

"She's not the type to put nasty flyers on people's windshields."

"Your judgment of women fails you again."

He kept tapping his book, as though he hadn't heard me. "Cassidy wouldn't have done it. She might have accidentally let the information slip to someone who could have done it, but she wouldn't have done it on purpose."

Typical Logan. He knew absolutely nothing about the situation, and yet he stood there defending Cassidy anyway. I said, "I'll let you know my opinion of Cassidy after our bet is over."

"You really think she was involved? Come on, Samantha, have you ever heard Cassidy even *say* a mean thing? I bet she doesn't have an enemy in the whole school."

I didn't say anything.

"She always helps people with their homework and stuff."

I didn't know whether he was trying to goad me into an insult or whether he was just smitten with Cassidy. I smiled graciously at him. "Go ahead and ask her out. You'd make a lovely couple."

"Naw, I think she's pretty tight with Josh Benson." He picked up the last of his books. "I'll stick with Veronica. After all, you'll never make it the next nine days without insulting someone."

I could have set him straight about Cassidy and Josh. He was bound to find out eventually that they'd broken up, and perhaps he'd back off this whole trying-to-get-me-to-insult-somebody thing if he knew Cassidy was available. But I didn't tell him. Somehow I didn't want to. I didn't want to see his face light up at the prospect of a date with her. I didn't want to endure Cassidy updates every time Logan and I were stuck working together. I refused to give him one more way to annoy me.

Instead, I said, "Not only will you have to take me to the Hilltop restaurant, but I'm going to make you hold the doors open for me and push in my chair."

He laughed and walked away. Even that was annoying.

For the next couple of hours, Logan and I didn't talk to each other. If I wasn't helping customers, then he was. When things finally slowed down, I walked over to the candy counter to see what I could buy that would substitute for real food. While I decided between a Milky Way and Corn Nuts, Doug walked in. I picked up the Milky Way and hoped he'd just pass by me, but he came and stood beside me. When I turned to go to the cash register, I nearly bumped into him.

"Hey, Samantha, you know chocolate is an aphrodisiac, don't you?"

"That must be why I love this job."

Instead of just wandering off somewhere, Doug stood beside me as I paid for my Milky Way. "Yeah, I bet it gets real boring in here, but hey, you look cute in that vest."

"Uh . . . thanks." I took the receipt and shoved it and the candy bar into my vest pocket. What I wanted to do was rip the wrapper off the Milky Way and gobble it down in two bites. But how could I do that with Doug standing there watching me? I walked back toward the books. Doug walked beside me.

"Is there anything in particular you're looking for?" I asked, remembering I should treat him like a customer.

"No, I just came in to browse." He took a quick survey of the store. "Hey, when do you get in the swimsuit edition of *Hot Babes* magazine?"

I looked at his face to see whether he was serious, but I couldn't tell. He wore a silly grin, which could have meant anything. "I don't know," I said. "I don't pay a lot of attention to *Hot Babes* magazine."

His grin got bigger. "Well, you work here. Aren't you supposed to know that kind of stuff?"

I forced a smile and tried to sound patient. "You're one of those guys who decorates his room using posters of scantily clad women draped over sports cars, aren't you?"

"Naw," he said, "I'm not much into sports cars." As we walked, he picked up a James Bond novel from the shelf and flashed the cover at me. It featured a woman wearing shorts that would have been tight on Thumbelina. "Now, *she'd* look good on a sports car."

I looked around for a customer, any customer who seemed like they might need help. Unfortunately, everyone milling around the store seemed completely content. Logan must have noticed my frantic gaze though, because he strode up to us with a big smile.

"Hey, Doug," Logan said happily. "What brings you into the literary world?"

"I was just passing by and thought I'd come in and say hi."

"He was checking to see if we had the swimsuit edition of *Hot Babes* magazine yet," I added.

Logan raised an eyebrow at Doug, but Doug just grinned. "Got to make sure I get mine before they're sold out. Which reminds me, when do you get next year's *Hot Babes* calendars in? I tried to get one last December, and they didn't have any."

Logan said, "Doug . . . ," and I thought Logan was about to comment on Doug's choice for marking the months, but the sentence disappeared and Logan's smile reappeared. "You like to get things done early," he said instead. "No procrastinating for you." Logan then glanced at me. "Isn't that a fine quality, Samantha?"

I matched Logan's cheery tone. "Almost as good a quality as respect for women."

Logan slapped a hand over Doug's shoulder. "And people who have calendars are organized and punctual."

"That is, if they ever look at the days part of the calendar," I said.

Doug was either tired of, or didn't understand, the direction the conversation had taken, so he broke in with the question, "So how late do you work here?"

I didn't know whether he was addressing Logan or me, but I was afraid it was me. Since I didn't want him to follow this question with any suggestions about getting together after work, I chose a vague answer, "The bookstore's open until seven P.M."

"But Mr. Donaldson doesn't make us close on school nights," Logan put in.

"Because he knows we have to go right home and do our homework," I added.

Doug tilted his head at me. "Do you do a lot of homework?"

I felt myself blush. Was he questioning my intelligence? Was he making some reference to my now famous SAT score?

"I need to start doing more," I said stiffly. "I'll let you guys talk. I have work to do."

I walked into the back room, sat down on one of the stools we used to reach the high shelves, and tore open my candy bar.

I would rather die than ever go out with Doug.

As I consumed mouthfuls of chocolate I wondered if Doug knew about the bet between Logan and me. Maybe that's why he'd spouted off about *Hot Babes.* Maybe he'd been trying to trick me into an insult.

But then again, it seemed entirely more likely that Doug was someone who saw women merely as good calendar material.

After I ate my candy bar, I straightened up the back room for a few minutes just so I wouldn't have to go out to the sales floor again. I stacked up all the stray books from the counter and was picking up pieces of trash from the floor when Logan came in.

"You can't hide in here forever," he said.

"Yes, I can." I saw the corner of a paper sticking out from underneath one of the shelves and bent down to pick it up.

Logan watched me for a moment, then sat down on the countertop and folded his arms. "He came all the way to the bookstore just to say hello to you. I thought it was very considerate of him."

The paper was stuck, and I ripped it as I pulled. "He actually said the words *Hot Babes* to me."

"So it would be good if you went out with him. You could enlighten him on the correct way to talk about women." He held up a peace sign. "You know, girl power and all of that stuff."

"Nine more days? I have nine more days until I can insult you again, right?"

"And I'm going to make it hard for you."

"You already are." I didn't wait for him to answer. I just walked out of the room and back onto the sales floor. I was half afraid Doug would still be lurking around someplace, but I didn't see him. Maybe he got tired of leering at the James Bond covers and went home.

I picked up a stack of books from the book cart and shoved them onto the shelf extra hard. Men. They had stupid calendars, and stupid bets, and stupid ways of driving, and stupid ways of breaking up with you, and stupid handwriting. The handwriting thought hurt the worst because it brought the whole flyer incident back to my mind. I'd been so busy worrying about retaliating, and then worrying about Doug, I forgot to worry about tomorrow when I'd have to face an entire student body who thought I couldn't spell SAT, let alone pass it.

Of course, I couldn't blame this horrible situation entirely on guys. After all, Cassidy had divulged my test score, and Amy had done the flyers, and they both belonged to my half of the population. It made the betrayal that much worse.

Next time I saw Cassidy, I'd tell her exactly what I thought of her and her supposed friendship, and then I'd—

Dang. That would fall under the insult category. If I hadn't been so dead set against going out with Doug, I would have blown the bet with gusto. I would have even invited Logan along to witness the event. As it was, the best thing to do would be to say nothing at all until the bet was over. Nothing now, and everything later.

I put the last of the books on the shelf and sighed. Nothing would be harder.

The next day at school was a trip to misery. Every time I walked down the halls, every time I sat at a desk, I felt the weight of a hundred stares on me. I told myself I was imagining it. Not *everyone* was watching me, not *everyone* was wondering about my intelligence.

Maybe.

Only a few people actually mentioned the flyers to me. Each time someone brought up the subject, I just shook my head like I thought it was funny and said, "Where do people come up with these rumors? Next they'll be saying I'm an undercover FBI agent watching for terrorist groups."

Whomever I was talking to would laugh, and then I'd say, "Just between you and me, the cafeteria ladies are scheming to take over the world."

More laughter. I'd join in. It's amazing how your face can do that while you want to cry.

I went from class to class and paid perfect attention to my teachers. I not only wanted to look studious, I wanted to be studious. I wanted to ace the SAT next time around and then photocopy the results and stick them to everyone's windshields; then we'd see if people ever believed Mr. Skinny *E*'s again.

After lunch the principal called Amy, Rick, and me into

the office to discuss the unsportsmanlike campaigning that had gone on the day before. She eyed Rick up and down from behind her desk with a dark expression. "If I knew for certain who made those flyers about Samantha and tore Amy's posters down, I'd disqualify him"—she snapped her fingers—"just like that. So whoever did it had better be watching himself very carefully, or he might just find himself out of the race and out of school." Then she glared at Rick again. It was enough to almost make me feel sorry for him. Almost.

We all swore we had nothing to do with any of it and promised to be model candidates. She let us go back to class.

Finally the day ended. I made it through all seven hours without bloodshed or a nervous breakdown. I was at my locker congratulating myself on this fact when Cassidy appeared beside me. She wore a pale blue sweatshirt and jeans. Chelsea would have called it simple, bland, and uncreative; and yet Cassidy still looked as though she'd just stepped out of an Ivory Soap commercial.

I hated girls who didn't struggle to be beautiful, and still were.

Cassidy leaned against the locker next to mine, holding a couple of textbooks against her chest, and nervously fingered the paper that stuck out of them. "Hi, Samantha."

"Hi."

She cleared her throat and shifted her weight from one foot to the other. "I just wanted you to know that Amy didn't make those flyers about you."

"Oh?" I shoved the last of my books into my backpack. "And why would you think I suspected her?"

She leaned in closer to my locker and lowered her voice. "Logan told me you thought I'd told Amy your test scores."

"Logan told you?" Great. Not only was he the thorn in my side but he had also become my publicist. Now, despite all of my attempts at humor and FBI jokes, it was bound to get around that those really were my test scores. Why did I tell anybody anything?

Cassidy shrugged. "Yeah, Logan was worried about you being upset."

"Uh-huh." Sure. Logan frequently agonized over my well-being.

"Anyway, I didn't tell anybody about your test score, but even if Amy had known about it, she wouldn't have made those flyers about you."

I slammed my locker door shut. "Oh. Well, that's very reassuring to know. I guess the Evil Flyer Fairy just visited our school parking lot then."

She blinked innocently. "Why are you so positive it was me?"

"Because you were the only one I told about my SAT score. I trusted you, Cassidy, and this is what I got."

She looked a little confused then, like she could see my logic but still didn't believe it. "Well, then someone must have overheard you telling me."

"Oh, yeah, probably one of the school hallway gnomes was listening."

She straightened up, and I could see every part of her stiffen. "I'm sorry you don't believe me."

"And I'm sorry about a lot of things." I turned and walked away.

. . .

This would have been a great parting line if I never had to see Cassidy again. Unfortunately, I had to see her that afternoon. I'd completely forgotten, until my mother reminded me, that I'd agreed to help out at the neighborhood fun fair.

Since Katya had arrived in Pullman, Cassidy's mom had done all sorts of fund-raisers to help out her old orphanage. One time she'd done a shoe drive. Another time all the women on our street got together to make quilts. On Halloween a bunch of kids went trick-or-treating for quarters to raise money for vitamins. Now it was the neighborhood fun fair.

Elise's fifteen-year-old brother, Dan, was actually supposed to be in charge of the event. He was counting it as his Eagle Scout project, but somehow the women of the neighborhood had taken over most of the organization, and my mother had recruited me to help out in the Jell-O toss booth. Kids were supposed to toss a little cube of Jell-O at a stack of dishes, and if it landed on one of the dishes, they got a prize. Kids love the idea of throwing food, but I was less than thrilled about helping. Somehow it was too easy to envision a bunch of kids with bad aim—or worse yet, kids with good aim—hitting me with the Jell-O cubes.

The fair had only one saving grace—they were holding it at the park located right next to Josh's house. If Destiny did her job, Josh would come out to the fun fair, run into me, and we'd spend a good portion of the afternoon talking and looking into each other's eyes. And then one thing would lead to another, and I'd casually ask him to take me to the prom.

Even to me it sounded like wishful thinking, and I hated having to depend on wishes to get things done. It would all be so much easier if Josh asked me out first, or at least seemed interested.

At the appointed time, Mom, Andy, Joe, David, and I all headed over to the park. My dad didn't come because he said he had to take his car in for an oil change and a tire rotation—like we couldn't see through that excuse. He just didn't want to get stuck in some booth where kids threw food at him.

My brothers were in charge of selling helium balloons, although from the way they were giggling in the backseat of the van, I knew they planned on sucking down half of the helium tank and singing Chipmunk songs the entire afternoon.

When we pulled up to the park, I noticed Cassidy and her mom unpacking paints and brushes for the face-painting table. Elise stood by the swings, pushing her three-year-old sister, Abby, and Katya back and forth in the air.

Cassidy *and* Elise. Even better. Dan was hovering over the baked-goods table, and Elise's parents were counting out tickets at the ticket booth. Josh, of course, was no where around. Destiny must have been on her lunch break.

I helped my mom tape numbers on the ground for the cakewalk, then went to a nearby picnic table to cut up the Jell-O for my booth. While I did this, Logan and his little brother drove up to the park in his ancient Toyota pickup. I recognized the oversized tires and two-toned, white and almost white, paint from where I stood.

Logan was constantly resurrecting his truck from the trash heap, and there probably wasn't an original piece of it left except the rearview mirror. But instead of being mortified to own such a piece of junk, Logan was constantly bragging about the improvements he'd made to it. While stacking books I'd heard more about engine capabilities than a person should have to endure in a lifetime.

I took out the first tray of Jell-O and sliced it into squares. Why was Logan here anyway? He didn't live in our neighborhood.

Maybe he was checking up on me. Any second now he'd come over and ask whether I'd made it through the day with my criticism in check. Then he'd ask me some insufferable question, like why, if they were so smart, women chose to pluck out their eyebrows or wear thong bikini underwear.

I kept one eye on him, but instead of coming in my direction, Logan and his brother walked over to where Dan stood.

Which must have meant Dan was friends with Logan's little brother and had asked them to help out. At least, I hoped Dan asked them to help out. I hoped Logan would be too busy to park himself in front of my booth and pelt me with Jell-O for the duration of the fair.

After Logan spoke with Dan for a few minutes, he left his brother and Dan and went over to where Cassidy stood.

Hmmm.

Maybe he was plotting something. Maybe he thought I'd be irritated if I saw him cozying up to Cassidy, and I'd be more likely to insult someone.

Or maybe he just liked her.

Oh, it was so irritating.

I sliced through the last of the Jell-O and piled the colored cubes onto plates. Every few seconds I looked over to where Logan and Cassidy stood. They were talking, standing close to one another, and laughing.

I wanted to claw her eyes out.

It was totally illogical to feel that way, but still I fumed.

Did I, or did I not, specifically tell Logan I didn't want him to date Cassidy? Well, okay, perhaps I actually said he *should* date Cassidy—that I thought they made a charming couple—but he knew I was being sarcastic when I said that. If he wanted to date someone, then he should go out with someone like . . . I tried for a moment to come up with an appropriate romantic choice for Logan, but couldn't think of anyone. I didn't dwell on it. After all, I wasn't interested in Logan. I'd come here to see Josh, or as it was turning out, to see the outside of Josh's house. Logan could date whomever he wanted. I wished them all the happiness in the world.

I threw the last of the Jell-O onto the plates as violently as I could, which of course did nothing but make the rest of the Jell-O stacks jiggle around a bit. It's hard to be violent with Jell-O.

I took the plates over to my mother and asked her what else needed to be done. She and Cassidy's mom had been talking, and now she surveyed the park. "It looks like we're about ready. I guess you can do whatever you'd like until the fair starts."

I glanced at my watch. We still had fifteen minutes left until the fair started. My choices were to wander around aimlessly, hang out with my little brothers, or barge in on Logan and Cassidy's conversation. Then I noticed my hands. Red streaks covered them from where I'd caught falling Jell-O. I really ought to wash them off, and what better place to do that than at Josh's house? If I trekked the three streets back to my house, I might be late getting back to the park, and I wouldn't want to disappoint all those kids who were eager to pelt Jell-O around. I was only thinking of them.

I walked over to the swings where Elise stood pushing the little kids and held up my hands. "Is it okay if I go in your house to wash my hands?"

"Oh, sure," she said. "Just walk right in." Then she smiled at me. A big friendly smile. One that should have set off warning bells.

I walked across the street to her house but paused on the doorstep. It felt odd to just walk into someone's house. I nearly rang the doorbell, but then thought that perhaps the reason Elise told me to go right in was because no one else was home. If I rang the bell, I'd look like an idiot standing on the porch waiting for someone to let me in. I looked back over my shoulder at Elise. She smiled again and made waving motions for me to go inside.

As daintily as I could so as not to get Jell-O on the doorknob, I opened the door and stepped inside. I had just shut the door behind me when a deep *"Woof!"* reverberated through the room and a mutatedly giant German shepherd strode toward me.

"Ah wahha!" I said, not because it made any sense, but because my vocal chords suddenly worked independently of my brain.

The dog barked two more times and then walked up to me, sniffing. Apparently he didn't get many visitors who smelled like raspberry Jell-O, and this was a treat for him.

Without taking my eyes from the dog, I took small steps back toward the door and called out, "Is anybody here?"

I had barely spoken the words when Josh walked into the room. He snapped his fingers at the dog. "Goliath!"

The dog turned around; wagged its tail with great, furry

sweeps; and trotted back to Josh. Josh looked down, but not very far down, at the dog. "Go into the kitchen," he said firmly.

Goliath immediately sat on the floor and gazed up at Josh as if waiting for the next command.

"All right then, sit!" Josh said. He turned and grinned at me. "Sorry if he scared you."

"I just came in to wash my hands." I held my hands up to show him the proof. "Elise told me to go right in."

Josh nodded, as though it was a natural occurrence for girls to appear in his living room. "Sometimes Elise forgets that people might not like our canine greeting committee."

I bet.

He showed me into the kitchen, and I tried to think of something intelligent to say while I washed my hands.

"You look older," I said, and wasn't sure why I'd chosen this. "I guess that's what happens."

"Yeah. You look older too."

The conversation was off to a roaring start. I turned off the water and smiled at him. Maybe I ought to take the direct approach. Maybe I ought to just say, "I have a problem, and I was wondering if you could help me out . . ."

"Are you going to the park, I mean the fair, you know, the thing outside?"

"Yeah, Dan put me in charge of the pie-eating contest." He nodded over to the counter, where several dozen pies were stacked up in rows. They were the store-bought kind that didn't look appetizing enough to eat at all, let alone scarf down in large quantities during a contest.

I let my hands drip into the sink while I looked around for a towel to wipe them on. I finally located one hanging from the refrigerator door and walked to it. Goliath saw me by the refrigerator and trotted over. With ears pricked, he watched me intently, as though I might be about to open the refrigerator and produce a ham for him.

Josh came over to pull the dog away from me again. He gave Goliath a push, then stepped between the dog and me. Josh was so close I could have thrown my arms around him if I'd wanted to. I wanted to, but I refrained. Instead, I said, "Do you need help carrying the pies out?"

"No, the pie-eating contest isn't going to happen for another hour or so." He didn't move away from the refrigerator—or from me. "That's nice of you to offer, though."

My hands were quite dry now, but I didn't move. "So what have you been doing since you got back to Pullman?"

"Mostly laundry."

"Oh. Fun."

And that pretty well exhausted my entire repertoire of small talk. I should have gone back outside instead of standing there staring at him. He was probably waiting for me to excuse myself, and yet I didn't go. "It sounds like you're ready for a break. Why don't you come outside now? I'll give you a discount on the Jell-O toss event."

He smiled, then looked down at his watch. "All right. I guess if I don't go out soon, Dan will accuse me of not supporting him."

The two of us walked to the front door. Goliath tried to follow us, but Josh shut the door on him before he could escape.

I heard Goliath bark sadly from behind the door, and when I glanced back at the house, he was standing at the entryway window, forlorn, with his nose pressed against the glass. It made me smile.

"He's kinda cute in a gargantuan type of way."

"He still hasn't forgiven me for going off to college. He doesn't want to let me out of his sight now."

Something Goliath and I had in common.

We walked down Josh's lawn, and as we did, Katya came running across the street toward us, with Cassidy close behind.

Just my luck. I'd had a total of four minutes alone with Josh, and now Cassidy arrived in the picture. Apparently Destiny was still out to lunch somewhere, downing curly fries and root beer instead of helping me with my love life.

Cassidy caught up with her sister just as she made it to the Bensons' lawn. She scooped up the little girl and very firmly said, "*Nyet,* Katya, a car could have hit you."

Elise and Logan crossed the street next, both out of breath, and joined Cassidy on the Bensons' lawn.

"That kid is fast," Elise said.

Katya wiggled in Cassidy's arms, then decided Cassidy's necklace merited interest and wound her fingers around it.

Josh walked over to the group, and I followed silently. He gazed at Katya in Cassidy's arms, and then at Cassidy.

"This is your new little sister? She's beautiful."

"Thanks." Cassidy said the word stiffly, looking at Katya and not at Josh.

Katya wriggled around some more, and Cassidy put her down. For a moment she looked as though she was going to sprint someplace else; then she noticed Goliath staring out the window. She cocked her head and studied him. "Bear!"

Cassidy glanced at the door. "No, Katya, that's Goliath. He's a dog."

"Bear," Katya said again, and walked toward him.

Elise chuckled and crossed her arms. "See, her English isn't so bad."

Josh watched Katya with the smile still on his face. "Does she know any sentences yet?"

Cassidy didn't answer for a moment, because she went to retrieve her sister before Katya could open the door and let Goliath out. Cassidy came back holding Katya in her arms. "She can say, 'I love you, Mama,' but that's because they taught her how to say it in the orphanage. I've been trying to teach her to say, 'I love you, Cassidy,' ever since we got her, but she just won't."

"Here, let me try." Elise held out her hands and took the little girl from Cassidy. She brushed Katya's hair away from her face and said, "Repeat, Katya, 'I love you, Cassidy.' "

Katya stared at her with wide, unblinking eyes and didn't say anything.

" 'I love you, Cassidy,' " Elise said again.

Katya put one hand on Elise's lips as though she wondered if it was possible to peel them off Elise's face.

Elise grinned, then handed Katya to her brother. "Here, Josh, you give it a try."

Josh glanced from Katya to Cassidy, then back to Katya. He cleared his throat and shifted his feet. "Say, 'I love you, Cassidy.' "

"Try it with feeling now," Elise said.

With a little more emotion he said, "I love you, Cassidy."

Elise smirked happily at him.

"Let me try." Logan held out his hands to Katya, and she came to him with a giggle. She clearly thought this was some funny American game people played at get-togethers.

In a voice that sounded like a dramatic actor's, Logan said,

"Repeat, 'I love you, Cassidy. I really, *really* love you. You are the *dearest* thing in my heart.' "

Katya laughed, but I wanted to slap Logan. To think that just days ago, he'd accused *me* of being an incurable flirt, and here he was performing a one-man love fest in Cassidy's honor.

I shouldn't have cared. After all, Logan was the most irritating guy alive. I should have hoped he hooked up with Cassidy. They deserved each other. But as Logan went on and on about his undying passion for her a knot of anger grew in my stomach. Finally Logan exhausted his expressions of love, and he looked over at me.

"She's not buying it from me," he said, and handed the little girl to me. "Why don't you give it a try?"

He probably thought I couldn't say anything to Cassidy at this point without throwing in a few insults. He was almost right. I gritted my teeth into a smile. " 'I . . . love . . . you . . . Cassidy.' "

Katya twisted around in my arms to look back at the Bensons' window. "Bear!"

Everyone laughed, and Cassidy reached over and took Katya from my arms. "I guess that's enough English lessons for now." Katya wound her arms around her sister's neck, and Cassidy held her close. Then Cassidy bent down and gave the little girl a kiss on the top of her head.

Josh and Logan both watched this display of sisterly affection with rapt attention. Logan even said, "Ohhh."

So. Apparently, all that time I'd spent studying fashion magazines to learn what attracted men had been a waste of time. What really got to guys was a girl who kissed her little sister. I had a sudden urge to say, "If any of my brothers had been a girl, I would kiss them."

Josh's gaze remained on Katya. He reached out and ran one finger across her cheek. "She really is beautiful."

Cassidy smiled, the stiffness falling away from her. "I think so."

Cassidy gave her sister another smile, then scanned the park. "Amy said she'd try to come today. If she's elected president, she wants to do something schoolwide to raise funds for Katya's orphanage. Isn't that neat?"

"Cool idea," Logan said, and then he—and everyone else—looked at me.

"I think that's a really good idea too," I said.

Logan tilted his head at me. "So what exactly are your political plans, Samantha? I mean, what are you going to do if you win?"

Leave it to Logan to put me in a tight spot. Suddenly I was supposed to come up with an idea better than helping orphans.

"I'd like to do service projects too," I said. "I haven't picked any specific ones yet; but, you know, giving money to the needy sounds like a good idea."

They continued to look at me, blatantly unenthusiastic about this suggestion, but really, what platform was I supposed to produce that would make everyone happy? Between keggers and orphans I just couldn't win.

The subject changed, and everyone went on talking except for me. No one seemed to notice I hadn't joined in, though, and I wasn't sure why I didn't. They suddenly seemed like such a tight-knit group. Only I was on the outside. I suppose I had always known this, but never cared before. Now it hurt.

For one moment I wondered what life would have been like if I'd been friends with Cassidy, Elise, and Logan. What if we were always together this way—what if I was always included in their circles?

Then I stopped thinking about it. It wasn't ever going to happen. Not now. Not ever. Not after those flyers.

From across the park Dan called, "Hey, you guys!" and waved for us to come over. Enough people had arrived, and he wanted to start the fair.

The booth went about like I thought it would. Most of the kids tossed—with varying degrees of success—their Jell-O onto the dishes. The littlest kids ate their Jell-O and then cried if I didn't give them a prize, and Joe's and David's friends all made a point of throwing their Jell-O at me and then pretending it was just bad aim. I took their quarters anyway and hoped the kids in Katya's orphanage appreciated my sacrifice for them.

Unfortunately, I didn't have another chance to talk to Josh. It was hours until one of Dan's friends relieved me from my Jell-O toss duties, and by then Josh had finished the pie-eating contest and was busy taking his littlest sister, Abby, around to the booths.

I got an overpriced piece of pizza from the refreshment stand and ate it on a grassy slope by the edge of the park. Logan walked over and sat down beside me just as I finished. "Hey," he said, stretching his legs out. "I thought I'd come and talk to you for a while."

"Oh, why?"

He picked up a grass blade and twirled it in between his fingers. "Oh, you know. Just to see how you're doing—and to ask you what you think of rap music, pro wrestling, and guys who pierce multiple parts of their body. That sort of thing."

I took the blade of grass from his fingers and shook it back at him. "It won't work. I have tremendous willpower, and I'm going to block out everything you say."

"So tell me, who do you think has more class, Brittany Spears or Eminem?"

Like I was going to fall for something that obvious. Still shaking the grass at him, I said, "What did you tell Cassidy about me?"

"When?" he asked, as though they'd had several conversations regarding me.

"When you told her that I thought she told Amy my SAT score."

"That was basically it," he said.

"Basically what?"

"Basically what I said."

I rolled my eyes. Was he trying to be difficult, or did guys just not know how to talk about things? I threw the blade of grass at him, and then because it wasn't enough, I grabbed another handful of grass and threw that at him too.

He said, "Hey!" and brushed the grass off his shirt, which of course was just an invitation for me to throw more at him. As I grabbed the second handful I told him, "This isn't an insult. I'm throwing this grass at you with the utmost respect."

After I'd christened him with the next handful, he retaliated with a few handfuls himself, and before long we were ripping up large chunks of the landscaping and flinging it at each other. He tried to rub some grass in my face, and I had to grab his hands to stop him. He pushed me over, and we probably would have had a full-blown wrestling match right there in the park if my mother hadn't suddenly appeared over us.

With a stern frown she looked down at us. "What are you two doing?"

Logan and I both sat up, mumbled apologies to her, and brushed the grass from our clothes. I noticed several people watching us, and I felt myself blush until they turned their attention back to the fair.

After my mom moved away, Logan mouthed to me, "You started it."

I stuck my tongue out at him, which technically wasn't an insult, since it involved no words.

He turned away from me, shaking his head; but just to show Logan I hadn't forgotten the subject at hand, I said, "So what did you tell Cassidy about me?"

He sighed and leaned back with his hands on the grass. "We were just talking, and I told her you thought she was involved with those flyers, and then she told me she hadn't told anyone your score results, which, if you recall, I told you all along."

"Right," I said. Because he might consider it an insult if I called him naive.

He smiled over at me. He had an even, gorgeous smile. One that always made him look like he was up to something. "It was your fault we were talking anyway, so you shouldn't be upset."

"My fault?"

"Yeah. As you know, I haven't had any luck with Veronica. So when I found out Cassidy wasn't going to the prom with anybody—well, it just seemed like a good idea to ask her."

"You asked Cassidy to the prom? Cassidy Woodruff?"

"She didn't do the flyers."

Yeah, yeah. He'd already professed her innocence. What I wanted to say was, *I thought we were friends. If you needed a date for the prom, why didn't you ask me instead of my archenemy?*

But that was a stupid thing to say. It was a stupid thing to even think. Logan and I at the prom—we'd probably end up wrestling on the punch table. Besides, I wasn't even sure Logan and I were actually friends. We were more like mutual nemeses.

I wanted to go to the prom with Josh. Josh, who was at this moment . . . I looked around the park until I located him. Josh, who was at this moment talking to Cassidy and Elise outside of the moon jump.

I just couldn't win.

Cassidy, apparently, could take whatever she wanted from me at will. The student body would probably put her in as a write-in candidate, and she'd win the school election too. It just wasn't fair.

I said, "Hey Logan, someone is moving in on your prom date. You'd better go defend your territory."

He looked over to where Josh and Cassidy stood talking, but didn't seem concerned. "I said we were going to the prom together, not getting married."

"Sure, you say that now. But you'll probably change your mind later."

He cocked his head and looked at me with a puzzled expression. I couldn't explain my last statement to him, so I smiled sweetly at him and changed my mind.

"On second thought, you'd better stay here with me. I feel like I'm on the verge of really, really insulting someone, and you wouldn't want to miss that." After all, I didn't want

Cassidy to think she could have Josh and Logan too. Since she was talking to my future prom date, I could sit here and talk to hers.

Logan nodded knowingly at me. "You're trying that reverse psychology stuff again, aren't you?" He leaned farther back, in a relaxed sort of way. "It won't work this time."

"Good. You're just too clever for me."

We sat and talked for the rest of the fair. Logan brought up every terrible topic he could think of, and I survived only by complimenting anyone and anything I felt like insulting.

"Daytime talk show hosts?" he asked.

"Snappy dressers," I answered.

He laughed a lot, and every time he did, part of me wanted to say, "See, you're having a good time with me. Why in the world did you ask Cassidy to the prom?" Then I'd want to smack myself for thinking that way.

It was just so ridiculous for me to have these thoughts about Logan when I wanted to be with Josh. And I did want to be with Josh. He was not only tall, dark, and handsome, he was mature and a little mysterious—and his fingernails never had car grease underneath them. Just to prove my point, I looked over at Logan's hands and noticed they were perfectly clean. How odd. When did Logan start taking care of his hands, and why hadn't I seen it before?

It didn't matter.

I was absolutely not interested in Logan in a romantic way. The guy had just told me he was going to the prom with Cassidy.

"School lunches?" Logan asked.

"Really, really nutritious," I said.

He tilted his head back in disbelief and groaned. I noticed that his hair stayed perfectly in place. He had great hair—so thick and wavy.

I wanted to smack myself again.

"Oh, I have it," Logan said. "The subject you can't resist insulting. Tell me, Samantha, what do you think about me?"

"Too much."

"Too much? What's that supposed to mean?"

Never mind what it means. I can't believe I just said it, and I'd never in a million years explain it to you. "No hablo inglés," I said. "Lo siento, señor."

"Don't think you can resort to insulting me in Spanish. I can spot an insult in any language."

"I bet you can. I'm sure you have a lot of experience in the matter."

"You're skating on thin ice," he said, and then with a smile added, "I knew you couldn't resist me."

But I did. For the rest of the night, in the recesses of my mind, I resisted him. I squelched any and every attraction I felt, and that was even harder than squelching insults.

After the fair was over, we packed up our minivan and headed home. The boys sat in the back shooting each other with plastic flying frogs they'd won at some booth, while Mom and I sat in the front and did our best to ignore them. Mom gave a contented sigh as we drove. "The fair went pretty well, don't you think?"

"Sure," I said, then ran my hand over my shirt, which was now blotched with red Jell-O.

"We cleared over three hundred dollars. Isabelle Woodruff

was thrilled. You know, she's so changed since they adopted Katya. She's always out and about, doing something with her. She's much happier."

I had never paid much attention to Mrs. Woodruff's level of happiness, so I just said, "Oh."

Mom glanced over at me. "Don't you think it's great that she's become so involved in helping kids?"

"Sure."

Mom's gaze returned to the street, but she shook her head. "There used to be a time you actually talked to me in sentences that involved more than one word."

This had been one of Mom's complaints against me lately. It wasn't enough to answer "fine" when she asked how my day had been. She wanted some sort of verbal essay.

I shrugged. "Sure, I think it's great that the Woodruffs are doing so much for the kids in Russia."

Mom didn't say anything for a moment, and I could tell she was deciding whether to drop the subject or not. I guess she decided in favor of dropping because when she spoke again, her voice returned to its normal tone. "So I noticed you and Logan Hansen spent a lot of time together tonight. What's going on between you two?"

"Nothing."

"Nothing?"

"Absolutely nothing."

"Right." Mom sighed and shook her head again. "You never tell me anything anymore."

The next day, instead of guy-ogling, my friends and I decided a campaign strategy meeting was in order. We went to the library, sat at a table in a remote corner, and rehashed all the events of the day before—who had said what about the flyers and about me, and how much all of this was likely to hurt my chances for election.

"It's worse than I thought," Chelsea said, pulling her chair closer to the table. "That flyer really boosted Amy's chances of winning the election. A lot of people think you can't be serious about being school president if you haven't been serious about your schoolwork."

Aubrie nodded. "And Rick has already captured the this-is-all-just-a-big-joke vote."

"You can't win on intellectual merit now," Chelsea said. "Your only hope is to try and present yourself as middle-of-the-road type of candidate. You know, not ultra-cerebral like Amy, but not a partyer like Rick."

"Okay. I'll be middle-of-the-road." I had no idea how to go about portraying that image. If I always walked down the center of the hallway, would people understand? "When I give my election speech, I'll try to sound really . . . average."

Rachel shook her head. "Not average, you need to be charismatic."

"Okay, I'll be charismatically in the middle of the road."

Aubrie said, "You never know—maybe you could turn the whole flyer incident to your advantage. People might see you as a victim and want to rally around you. Try to play on that."

"I'll be a charismatic middle-of-the-road victim," I said.

"And remember to appear dedicated," Rachel added.

I gripped the edge of the table. "My head will explode if you give me any more directions."

"You're doing fine. Just try to act presidential," Aubrie said.

The explosion felt imminent. "And how am I supposed to do that?"

Chelsea patted my hand as though I were a child. "There's no need to get upset. Everything will work out. Let's change the subject."

No one said anything for a moment, and then Aubrie asked, "So, do you have any new prospects for the prom?"

The prom. Now there was a subject. I traced the lettering on my English 315 book, looking at it instead of my friends. I wanted to ask Josh to go with me, but I wasn't sure I had the courage to mention the subject to him, let alone ask him to rent a tux and take me.

"I kind of like this one guy," I said slowly. "But I'm not sure if he's interested in me."

"Oh, I think he's interested," Rachel said.

I blinked at her in surprise. "What?"

"I think it's pretty obvious that Logan likes you."

"Logan? What makes you think I was talking about Logan?"

My friends passed a knowing glance around the table, and then Aubrie said, "Well, the two of you *are* pretty obvious about it."

"We are not," I squeaked out. "Logan and I are definitely not obvious, I mean interested. I mean—well, you know what I mean."

"Oh, come on," Chelsea said. "You two are always talking with each other in the hallways."

"That's because of his diabolical bet. Not because I like him."

Rachel smirked at me. "Then why do you two always stand so close together when you talk?"

"We don't."

"You do too," Aubrie said.

"Then that must be because the hallways are crowded or something."

"Uh-huh," Chelsea said. "You also laugh when you're around him."

"I find parts of his personality amusing."

"And what do you find the other parts?"

I tapped my fingers against my English book, trying to think of the right way to phrase how I felt about Logan. "He's just one of those people that I . . . put up with. And besides, he asked Cassidy Woodruff to the prom."

"Ohhh," Chelsea said, as if she understood everything perfectly now.

"But I wasn't talking about Logan anyway. I was talking about Josh Benson. He's back from college, and I've run into him a couple of times. I'm thinking about asking him to the prom."

My friends looked at me silently. Finally Aubrie said, "As a revenge type of thing because Logan asked Cassidy?"

"No, not for revenge. This has nothing to do with Logan. Just forget Logan. I like Josh. I just don't know how to casually ask him to the prom."

"Don't do it casually," Chelsea said. "Come up with some cute idea he won't be able to turn down—like a singing telegram or something."

Rachel rested her elbows on the table and leaned toward me. "My sister asked a guy out by putting cinnamon rolls in a toy dump truck, and then she attached a note that said, 'I'd like to haul your buns to the Sadie Hawkins.' "

Aubrie nodded. "My cousin asked her date to Sadie Hawkins by stapling a pair of Superman underwear to a poster and then writing on it, I'LL BE BRIEF, COME WITH ME TO THE DANCE."

Chelsea hit her hand against the table as though she'd thought of the perfect idea. "A baby chicken in a basket with a note that says, 'This chick would love to go to the prom with you.' "

"Good ideas," I said, "but somehow I can't see myself giving Josh underwear, live poultry, or anything that references his rear end."

"You'll think of something," Chelsea said. "There are hundreds of cute ways you can ask him."

The first bell rang, and we got up to go to our classes. As Rachel tucked her books under her arm she said, "Do an invitation with candy. Guys love to eat."

I thought about it as I walked to class, and with each step my spirits rose. Chelsea was right. There were hundreds of cute ways to ask Josh to the prom, and guys didn't turn down cute invitations, did they? Besides, if I gave him a Candygram, I wouldn't have to face him while I asked him out. Definitely a plus.

Throughout the day I thought of various ideas I'd heard about over the years. I finally decided to buy bags of Mounds, Big Hunks, bubble gum, and Starbursts. I would spread them on his bedroom floor and tape some to a note that read, "It would be Mounds of fun to go to the prom with a Big Hunk like you. I'm Bursting to know your answer. Don't blow it, and give me a call." Then I'd leave my name and phone number.

The hard part would be arranging a time when I could go to his house to set up the invitation. I didn't want to call his mother, tell her what I was planning, and ask permission to come into his house to do it, but what choice did I have? I absolutely wasn't going to ask Elise to let me in.

Besides, maybe his mother would become my ally in the affair. I could almost see her telling him, "You're not going to turn down Samantha, are you? She's such a nice girl and went to all of that work . . ."

I called her when I got home from school, explained the situation, and asked when Josh would be gone so I could come over.

"He'll be at the store until seven tonight," she said. "The rest of us will be in and out all evening. Elise will be at drama practice . . ."

She said more, but my mind stopped on the Elise at drama practice part. It was perfect timing. Elise wouldn't be around to harass me while I spread candy on the floor.

She ended her statement with, "so someone should be

here to let you in, but if not, I'll leave the door unlocked. Josh's room is the first door on the left, at the top of the stairs."

"Um . . . your dog?"

"I'll make sure he's in the backyard so he doesn't bother you." She sounded distracted while she said all this, as though her mind had already shifted to the upcoming plans for the evening, so I worried she might forget about this little detail. Then instead of a cute prom invitation, Josh would find my mangled corpse on his floor.

But as I walked up to the Bensons' front door, gripping my bags of candy in case I needed to use them as a weapon, I heard Goliath barking in the backyard. Josh's mom had remembered.

No one answered the bell, so I self-consciously opened the door and made my way to Josh's bedroom. It was strange standing alone in his room, looking at the memorabilia on his dresser and seeing the hamper with his clothes. It all seemed so intimate. So personal. I put my stuff down on his bed and resisted the urge to open his drawers to see what he kept in there.

Tape. I needed to tape the note somewhere. The dresser mirror? The closet door? If I opened his closet, I could run my fingers across the shirts he'd be wearing all next week.

I ripped off a piece of tape and stuck it on the back of my note. I needed to do this and leave fast. I'd only spent a few minutes in Josh's room, and already I was thinking like a stalker. Besides, what would I do if someone came home and found me inside of Josh's closet caressing his T-shirts? I pressed the note on the floor and taped candy onto it. Then I popped a Starburst into my mouth while I decided how to arrange the rest of the candy on the floor.

A heart? Too mushy. Scattered haphazardly? Too boring. An arrow would work. I got down on my hands and knees and formed the candy into the tip of an arrow pointing at the note, then I scooted backward, creating a tail. It was a long tail because I'd bought so much candy, and by the time I'd finished, it stretched out of Josh's room into the hallway.

Oh, well. It sort of looked like it was supposed to do that—as though I'd been planning to give him a clue about what was coming even before he reached his bedroom.

I picked up my things and, feeling a bit like I was Goldilocks, hurried out before any bears could catch me.

For the rest of the evening, while I tried to do my homework I listened for the phone to ring.

7:15 Certainly he was home by now. Why hadn't he called?

7:30 Maybe he hadn't gone upstairs to his room yet. Maybe he was one of those guys who liked to come home, eat, and unwind in front of the TV.

7:45 Okay. Maybe he was still in front of the TV, but wasn't anybody else home yet? Hadn't anyone noticed my candy arrow and called down, "Hey Josh, you might want to come upstairs and check this out."

8:00 Maybe Elise had come home and done something diabolical to my invitation. I wouldn't put it past her.

8:15 Maybe he wasn't calling because he just didn't want to go to the prom with me.

8:30 He was probably now rehearsing his speech about how he'd decided to become a monk and had thus given up dating.

8:45 Josh hated me and wasn't even going to give me the benefit of a poorly thought out and obviously transparent excuse. I would never hear from him again.

At 9:00 the doorbell rang, and Mom called out, "Samantha, there's someone here to see you."

I padded down the stairs and found Josh waiting by the front door. His hair was tousled, as though he'd been running his fingers through it (or trying to rip it out?), and he wore a beleaguered expression. (He was having a hard time coming up with even a transparent excuse?)

"Hi, Samantha," he said slowly.

"Hi, Josh." I gripped the edge of the banister. If it couldn't be painless, I hoped it would at least be quick.

"Sorry it's taken me so long to get back to you. I had to take my dog to the vet."

Of course, why hadn't I thought of that before? Usually, when a guy doesn't call you at 7:00 P.M., it's because he's taking his dog to the vet. Those are the vet's busiest hours.

And then a horrible thought slammed into me. In my mind I could suddenly see my candy arrow on Josh's floor and Goliath loping toward it. All of that candy—and put so conveniently at dog level. "Um, why did you have to take your dog to the vet?"

"Well, he sort of ate your invitation."

"He ate it? All of it?"

"Not your note, but it was kind of hard to read after he threw up on it."

"He threw up on it?" I suddenly had a flashback to Frisky in Brad's car. Another animal had vomited on my love life—and this time it was my fault. Why hadn't I just chosen the underwear invitation instead?

"Chocolate is pretty hard on a dog's system," Josh said tiredly. "And those little plastic wrappers don't help."

"He ate the wrappers too?" It was a stupid question. What had I expected—that Goliath had sat down and unwrapped each piece with his paws? "I am so sorry."

"It's not your fault. My mom was the one who let him inside, and she knew about the candy on the floor. She just didn't think Goliath was stupid enough to eat it." His eyes got a faraway look. "Although you'd think she'd have known better after last year, when he ate Abby's entire Polly Pocket village."

"Goliath ate a village?"

"It was made up of miniature marshmallows glued to cardboard. We never did recover Polly. The vet said she would come out of Goliath eventually, but there are some things you just don't want to search through."

"I'm so sorry," I said again. "Is Goliath going to be all right?"

"Yeah. Although you don't want to be around a ninety-pound dog on a sugar high."

"I'm so sorry." And then because the three times I'd already said it didn't seem like enough—"I'm really sorry."

The faraway look faded from his eyes, and Josh seemed to remember he was standing in my house. "About your note. I couldn't actually read it, but my mom said it was from you. What did it say?"

Which meant I was going to have to ask him to the prom face-to-face anyway. I swallowed hard and tried to say the words as if they formed any other sentence. "The note said, 'It would be Mounds of fun to go to the prom with a Big Hunk like you. I'm Bursting to know your answer. Don't blow it and give me a call.'" And although it had been cute when written in Candygram form, it sounded really stupid when you said it out loud.

"Prom?" He looked at me with uncertainty.

Uncertainty is not the facial expression you want to see a guy wear when you've just asked him out, and I started to prepare myself for the latest round of rejection from Josh.

I was still second-best. Or worse yet, I was third or fourth, or perhaps even in the only-if-you-were-the-last-woman-on-earth category.

Josh said, "But aren't you going out with Logan?"

"Logan?"

"Yeah, I thought you two were a couple."

"We're not dating. Why would you think that?"

He shrugged. "I don't know. I guess every time I see you, you're hanging out together."

Well, that explained why he never flirted back with me. He thought I was taken. Now that this little misconception was cleared up, everything would be different between us.

I tried not to blush. "No, I'm not seeing anyone right now."

"Oh." Josh cracked a small smile, and I wondered if I was blushing despite myself. "Well, then I'd be happy to go with you."

We discussed the details, the day and time—that sort of

thing, and all the while I kept hearing his sentence, "I'd be happy to go with you."

He was happy. And I was blissful.

On Friday morning, as I dropped a bagel into the toaster for breakfast Mom walked into the kitchen and leaned against the counter.

"We need to have a talk."

A talk. Oh, no. Those were always bad words when they came from a parent's mouth. Before I could say anything, Mom went on. "During our post-fair meeting Isabelle Woodruff told me she was sorry to hear about the flyers somebody made about you. She asked me how you were doing." Here, Mom tapped her fingers on the counter in a quick, angry rhythm. "I of course had to tell her I had no idea what she was talking about."

My bagel popped up, but I didn't reach for it. At the moment it wasn't the only thing that was toast.

"Why didn't you tell me about those flyers?" Mom went on. "I mean, somebody at school spreads vicious rumors about you, and you don't even mention it in passing to your parents? We care about you, Samantha. These are the type of things we want to know about."

Vicious rumors. The words rang in my ears. I opened my mouth to say something, but nothing came out. How could I now, how could I ever, tell her the truth? Finally I stuttered out, "It was just campaigning stuff. Everyone expects that kind of thing."

"Well, I hope you marched right into the office and complained."

I took the bagel out of the toaster and put it on my plate, even though I didn't feel hungry anymore. "I took care of it."

"Anyone who does that sort of campaigning ought to be thrown out of the race."

I didn't say anything. I just dipped my knife into the butter and slowly spread it across my bagel.

Mom looked off into the distance and shook her head. "Of course I let everyone know those flyers weren't true. I told them that you hadn't even got your test scores back yet. Eight ten. Honestly." Now Mom looked back over at me. "Maybe it will come today."

"Maybe." If someone at the SAT board had a really cruel sense of humor and sent a second copy, that was.

In art class the teacher told us to find a magazine picture that depicted an emotion and draw it. While I was in the supply room flipping through a *Better Homes and Gardens,* Elise and Cassidy came in. Elise dropped a stack of magazines beside me, then leaned up against the counter. "So tell me, Samantha, when you asked Josh to the prom, were you trying to kill our dog or just ruin our carpet?"

I looked at my magazine, and not at her. "How was I supposed to know your dog would eat my invitation? It's not like I spelled it out in Alpo."

"Some people use the phone to hold conversations. It's cleaner that way."

I refrained from an insult. It took superhuman powers.

Cassidy turned a page of her magazine with such force she nearly ripped it in half. "You know, Samantha, I really had nothing to do with those flyers. You didn't have to go and . . . ," but she didn't finish her sentence. She just flipped over another page.

"Go and what?" I asked.

"Go and do things to purposely upset me."

"I didn't ask Josh out to upset you."

Elise ignored me and nodded knowingly at Cassidy. "See,

it wouldn't bother you that Samantha is throwing herself at Josh if you were really over him. This proves it."

"This doesn't prove anything," Cassidy said.

"I'm not throwing myself at Josh," I said. "I just asked him to a dance."

Cassidy rolled her eyes.

"See," Elise told Cassidy. "Admit it. You're upset."

"I am not upset," Cassidy said, then to me added, "If you want to ask him out, fine. Marry him for all I care."

Elise turned to me and in a lower voice said, "It won't do you any good to keep chasing Josh. He likes Cassidy. He always has."

"Thanks for the warning," I said sweetly. If Josh and I ever did get married, I definitely wouldn't ask Elise to be a bridesmaid.

After lunch Logan came up to me while I got my biology book from my locker. He'd made a habit of checking up on me in between classes, and as he leaned against the locker next to mine he said, "I hear you and Josh Benson are going to the prom."

"Yep." I wanted to see a twinge of jealousy on Logan's face, but he only nodded. "So what ever happened to you and Brad?"

As if he didn't know. By now the entire junior class knew how Brad had dumped me. I just smiled at Logan. "It didn't work out."

"But you still think fondly of Brad anyway, right?"

"I think it would be fond if Brad—" I stopped myself only a moment before I blurted out an insult.

He broke into a big grin. "I almost had you there."

I shut my locker door with a thud. "You know, you really ought to give up this silly bet because I doubt you're Veronica's type."

"Why not?"

"Because you're a—" I stopped myself again, and then simply shook my head to show him I wasn't speaking to him any longer. I leaned against my locker and waited for him to leave, but he stayed where he was, watching me.

His eyes actually twinkled. It was odd, it really was, how jovial he'd become since our wager. It was like tormenting me had become the most fun thing in his life. "You still have one more long week until you're able to insult me," he said. "Why not just give up now and save yourself the inner turmoil?"

"You're the one who ought to give up this bet. Do you know what people are saying about us?"

He shrugged. "That we're the gambling sort?"

"No. That we like each other."

He tilted his face back in astonishment. "Why?"

"Because we're always talking to each other, and because—look, you're doing it right now."

"Doing what?" he asked with real alarm.

"You're standing too close to me."

He looked at where I stood and then down at his own feet. "What's wrong with the way I'm standing? I'm at least two feet away from you."

"Yeah, but you're leaning toward me."

"Only because you speak so softly, and besides, you're leaning toward me too."

I hadn't noticed it before, and now I straightened up, but just a little. "You're either going to have to stop walking me to class every day or do the honorable thing and ask me out, because otherwise people will think you're just toying with my affections."

"Toying with your affections?" He out and out guffawed. "No one would think that."

"Josh and my friends all told me they thought we had something going on."

"That's only a few people."

"If my friends think it, then other people do too . . ." I shrugged a bit uncomfortably. "If for no other reason than my friends don't keep their opinions to themselves."

Logan crossed his arms, but didn't move away from me. "Well, then tell your friends to stop spreading wild rumors about our love life."

As Logan said this, two guys from our class rounded the corner and walked close by us. They looked at us with raised eyebrows, and one snickered, but neither said anything.

I waited until they'd passed, then whispered to Logan, "See, there go two more misinformed people. And by the way, you're leaning toward me again."

He stood up straight and took a step away from me. "I am not, and those guys are only misinformed because I just said that stuff about our love life."

"Exactly my point. You have to stop doing that kind of thing."

For a moment he looked like he didn't know what to say, and then he shook a finger at me. "You're only saying all of this because you don't want me to be around you at school—because you know if I talk to you, you're going to lose our bet."

"I just think it would be better because of all the gossip if you didn't hang around me for a while . . . say a week."

"Not a chance. I'm going to be your second shadow." And then he took two steps toward me and purposely leaned over until he was almost touching me.

I'm not sure why, but I felt myself blush. I hadn't been this close to Logan since the eighth grade. If I reached out my fingertips just a bit, I could touch his hand. I had held his hand once at a junior-high dance, but the funny thing was, it had never made me blush back then.

I couldn't help my smile. "If you'd just stop hanging around me for a while, I'm sure I'd let my guard down and slip up."

"No way. I'm sticking so close to you that by the end of the week the rumor mill will have predicted our engagement date, named our children, and picked out the family dog."

As we walked together to the cafeteria I kept telling Logan he should leave me alone for the next week, and he kept insisting he wasn't going to leave my side. Which, somehow, didn't seem all that bad of an arrangement.

You know, I'd never put much stock in reverse psychology, but suddenly, suddenly I'd gained a newfound respect for the idea.

On Monday a girl from the journalism class took the candidates' pictures for the school newspaper. She also asked each of us what our main goal as president would be. I said I wanted to promote school unity.

Amy said she wanted to organize class projects, and then went on to explain our need to be financially solvent and our obligation to provide community service. Technically, I thought this counted as listing more than one goal, but the reporter busily wrote it all down anyway. I wished I'd come up with something that could have branched off into other goals like Amy had, because it made her sound like she had an active agenda planned, which, come to think of it, she probably did.

Rick said if elected president his main goal would be to change our mascot to something besides a greyhound because greyhounds are skinny little dogs that other dogs would beat up if they could. No one, Rick insisted, is afraid of greyhounds; so he thought we should be, like, the Pullman High deranged postal workers. Classic Rick.

All through the week Logan was good to his word about being my shadow. I saw him at lunch, twice between classes, and after school. On Wednesday and Thursday I saw him not only at school but at work too. He was frequently at my side asking questions. "Do we have any more copies of that great Wrestlemania book in stock?" or "Do you think it's too early to remind Mr. Donaldson to order the *Hot Babes* calendars?"

I wasn't even tempted into uttering an insult, though. I actually liked all the attention he gave me. After all, he was Cassidy's prom date, and he was ignoring her and by my side every free moment. Who wouldn't like that? And all of the extra time I took to choose my clothes and do my hair, well, that was just because of the campaign.

On Friday, just to annoy Logan, I called him some term of endearment every time I saw him. I also constantly reminded him this was the last day of our wager.

"Three more hours until our bet is through, darling," I told him as we walked together to lunch.

He sighed. "I know."

"You'll just have to kiss the thought of Veronica good-bye."

"I know."

"She wasn't good enough for you anyway, snookums."

"Yeah, yeah."

"Have I mentioned when you take me out, I'll be ordering several appetizers?"

"Six or seven times."

"See you after next period, O devoted one."

I sat down at my table, and Logan walked over to the one where he sat. As I took the sandwich from my lunch sack my friends all stared at me icily.

"What?" I asked.

"'O devoted one'?" Chelsea said. "We've sunk to 'O devoted one'?"

"And I thought all those perky 'have-a-nice-day' comments were annoying," Rachel said.

I held my sandwich up and nibbled on the crust. "It's the last day of the bet. I'm going to wait until three o'clock and then tell Logan my opinion on everything from his taste in women to rap music."

Chelsea rolled her eyes. "Just be back to normal when we see you tomorrow, okay?"

"Oh, definitely," I said. "I'll be as normal as ever."

After school I waited by Logan's locker. As he picked up his books I stared at my watch and gave him the countdown. "Fifteen minutes and thirty-five seconds left until our bet is over. Fifteen minutes and ten seconds until our bet is over."

"I can't wait around for the outcome," he said. "You'll just have to let me know how it turns out."

"What do you mean you can't stick around? You've been

positively following me around for two weeks, and now you're not going to stick it out for the next—" I looked back at my watch—"fourteen minutes and fifty-two seconds?"

"I've got errands to run. Cassidy and I are doubling with Elise and Tyson, so Tyson and I have to pick up our tuxes. But I'll see you tomorrow night. You can rub it in then."

"Oh." I wasn't sure why his answer stung. "Well, why don't you just concede the bet now then? You know you're a loser."

His mouth dropped open. "I'm a what?"

"That wasn't an insult, just a prediction on the outcome of our bet."

"Samantha, you're such a cheater."

"Tell it to the lobster," I said, and walked away.

On Saturday I took off work so I could help the rest of the decorating committee turn the PHS cafeteria into a ballroom with ambience. We brought in silk trees and set up a fountain in the corner. We intertwined angel hair and ribbons along the railings. I personally tacked up twinkle lights from one end of the room to the other. I even had my dad come in and help me wire them across the ceiling so they'd look like stars.

At six o'clock Josh picked me up for dinner. He stood in my living room, looking like he'd just stepped off a billboard advertising gorgeous men, and pinned a corsage of pink roses on my dress. Then I fumbled to pin the boutonniere on his lapel without impaling him while my parents took at least a dozen pictures to memorialize the event.

Finally, we left the photo shoot and went to dinner at Basilos. While we ate, I learned Josh was studying premed at college. Very impressive. He'd actually be able to afford that villa in Spain. He asked me about school, and it's funny because every once in a while I wanted to complain about the teachers or some of the kids that went to PHS, but I didn't. I just couldn't bring myself to. It was like the last two weeks of never insulting anyone had rubbed off on me, and it still felt unnatural to say anything bad about anyone. I was afraid Logan would jump out from somewhere, point a finger at me, and scream, "Aha!"

Logan. He would laugh if he knew what he had done to me with his silly bet. And he'd laugh if he knew I was sitting here with my prom date thinking of him. I'm sure wherever he and Cassidy were, he wasn't thinking about me.

Josh took a sip of water from his glass, but then instead of picking up his fork again, he smiled over at me. "You've really changed since last year."

"Oh?" This was the part where he would tell me he'd been a fool, that he should have dated me instead of Cassidy—that I wasn't second-best.

"Last year . . ." He shrugged, as though he wasn't sure how to explain. "You were so cynical."

"Cynical?"

"You were always criticizing everyone."

I just stared at him, a terrible lump forming in my stomach.

He must have thought my staring meant I didn't understand him. "I mean, I'm glad you've changed, because being around critical people always makes me nervous. I figure it will only be a matter of time before they start criticizing me."

I wanted to tell him, *You can stop elaborating now. I get it. You thought I insulted people. You probably thought I couldn't go two weeks without insulting someone.*

Logan had been right about me. Oh, that hurt.

So I wouldn't have to say anything for a moment, I took another bite of my dinner. I tried to console myself with the resolve that I would change. From now on, I'd be a kinder, gentler Samantha. I hadn't insulted anyone for over two weeks, and I could continue my streak. Then the compliment Josh had paid me would be true. I wanted it to be true.

I smiled back at Josh. "I wouldn't think you'd have to worry about anyone being critical of you. I mean, what's to criticize?"

He laughed and said, "You obviously haven't spent a lot of time talking to Elise about me, have you?"

"Nope."

He picked up his fork, but then paused. "You guys didn't really get along last year, but I could never figure out why that was."

The old me would have volunteered several reasons, starting with the fact that I'd heard Elise, on more than one occasion, call me "her royal blondness," but the new me refrained. I just smiled and shrugged like I too thought it was a mystery.

After dinner we drove to the high school for the Cinderella-like portion of the evening. As we went up the school steps I just knew magic awaited us on the dance floor. Josh would hold me close, look into my eyes, and everything would be perfect.

As we walked into the lobby, music filled the air and I could smell the soft scent of rose petals all around me. Actually, the prom committee had bought a dozen Springtime Bouquet air fresheners and placed them around the room. But the effect was the same—I breathed in the sweet smell of romance.

I took Josh's arm as we walked toward the dance floor. I had arrived at the ball.

It felt strange to dance to rock music in a formal dress. I almost felt like we should waltz or something; but no one else seemed to feel uneasy, and so after a few minutes I didn't either.

Usually when I dance with a guy, he looks at me, but Josh

kept peering around the room. Probably taking a trip down memory lane. The next song came on, and he still kept glancing around every few seconds. Probably appreciating all the work I'd put into the decorations.

Or maybe he was searching for someone.

I got my answer when Cassidy and Logan walked into the room. Josh's gaze went to her—and stayed there for several moments.

True, she did look pretty. She wore a flowing baby-blue dress, and her hair was piled on the top of her head with little pink roses tucked in here and there. Sophisticated and innocent. Even Chelsea would be impressed. Josh was probably only staring at her because she looked so different than she usually did. In a moment his attention would return to me. Certainly.

In the meantime, I stole a glance at Logan. Standing there in his tux, he looked taller, older, handsome. He took Cassidy's arm, smiled down at her, and led her to the dance floor.

The song ended, and a slow one followed. Josh gently pulled me into his arms. I had been awaiting this moment, but somehow it didn't make me feel tingly. It just made me feel like we were now in slow-dance position. I kept wondering if he was watching Cassidy over my shoulder.

I tried to change the subject, even though we hadn't been talking. "I don't suppose the school is much different than it was when you were here last year."

"No, not unless the twinkle lights are a permanent addition."

"Hey, don't make fun of my twinkle lights. I stood on a ladder for two hours this morning putting those things up."

He laughed just a little. "You did a good job with the

decorations. You're very dedicated. You'll make a good president."

"You really think that?"

"Sure."

"Elise and Cassidy are campaigning for Amy Stock." I'm not sure why I said this. I suppose I wanted him to know the truth about Cassidy and to stop staring wistfully at her.

Instead, he immediately turned and looked at her again. "Really? Why?"

I wanted to say, *Because she isn't my friend. Because she's vindictive and mean.* Instead, I shrugged. "I guess it's just one of those things."

My friends would truly be disappointed at how far my scathing commentaries had sunk.

Josh squeezed my hand lightly, sympathetically. "I'd vote for you if I could."

"Thanks." I felt a little better.

At least I felt a little better until the next time he glanced over at Cassidy. And the next time after that. And the time after that.

By the time we'd danced through a couple more songs, my jaw was clenched so tight I probably looked like the prom version of the nutcracker. Prince Charming, I was sure, never looked at someone else while he was dancing with Cinderella. I thought back to our conversation at the restaurant. "What could anyone criticize you for, Josh?" I'd asked.

Suddenly the answer to that question was becoming very clear.

What was it with him? Was Cassidy so bewitching, or was I just so uninteresting? Instead of proving I was no longer second-best, he was positively confirming it. I was torn between wanting to fight for his attention and wanting to kick him in the shins.

When the next song ended, I said, "I'm a little thirsty. Do you want to go get a drink?"

"Sure." We walked over to the refreshment table together; but he didn't take my hand, and I didn't take his. We picked up a couple of sodas and some heart-shaped sugar cookies, then walked up to the landing, where rows of tables and chairs waited. The music didn't seem so loud here, but we could still see everybody on the dance floor.

I sunk down into a chair, and Josh sat down beside me. He took a slow drink of soda. I broke my heart cookie in two. Mrs. Mortenson, my English teacher, would have found that quite a symbolic thing to do. She had been lecturing us lately about symbolism and was such an expert on the matter that I'm sure she could have found meaningful symbolism in the ingredients list of a box of crackers. I nibbled on one end of the cookie. Also symbolic. Eat your heart out.

And then I laughed a little. Usually I couldn't keep my mind off guys during English class. Now, here I was out on a date thinking of literary terminology. What a good example of situational irony.

Josh looked over at me questioningly, but I didn't explain myself. If he wanted me to share my thoughts, then he could at least pay attention to me for two consecutive minutes.

After a few moments of silence he said, "So how are the sports teams doing this year?"

"About the same. We win some; we lose some."

He nodded. "That's good." Then he glanced over at Cassidy again.

I had to quell the urge to say, "If you want to rest your eyes for a while, I'll take a turn staring at her."

We finished eating the rest of our cookies in silence; then because he probably couldn't think of any more small talk, he said, "Do you want to dance some more?"

"Sure."

We both got up and walked toward the dance floor. Elise, Tyson, Cassidy, and Logan stood together at the edge of the floor talking, and as we walked near them Elise waved at us to come over.

Josh walked over to her, and I followed him. "Hey," he said. "How are you guys doing?"

"Wonderful as always," Elise replied.

I didn't mean to end up standing next to Logan, but somehow it happened. He looked me over with a smirk I couldn't interpret.

I wanted to talk to him, but not in front of this group. I listened to Elise, Josh, and Tyson talk for a minute. When I was sure no one was watching Logan or me, I glanced over at him. The moment I did, he returned my gaze. I leaned closer to him and whispered, "I won our bet, you know."

"Congratulations."

"I'm free next Saturday night."

"All right. I'll pick you up at six."

I smiled and turned back to the rest of the group. I should have felt a little bit guilty about arranging one date in the middle of another, but I didn't. I just looked attentively over at everybody and pretended to follow the conversation.

Logan leaned over and whispered in my ear, "Is that all you have to say?"

"What do you mean?"

Still whispering, he said, "I thought you had a bunch of backlogged insults to tell me."

"Oh, yeah." I thought for a moment and then said, "Rap music is awful, Freud was weird, and Doug Campton needs to grow up."

"What about me?"

"You're annoying."

"That's it? That's your backlog? After two whole weeks?"

"I'm just not a cynical or critical person." I only blushed slightly as I told him this. "Even Josh said so."

And this was the point that Josh decided to tune into our conversation.

"What did I say?" he asked.

I didn't want to repeat any part of the conversation, so I just pretended I had no idea what he was talking about. I gave him a slightly confused look and repeated, "What did you say?"

"I said, 'What did I say?' " Josh answered.

I blinked at him a couple of times. "I give up. What *did* you say?"

I could tell Josh was weighing whether or not it was worth trying to clarify things when Elise chimed in. "I know what you said. When we were back home, you said you'd save me a dance." She held out her hand to him. "They just started one I like. Let's go."

Josh turned to me apologetically. "I did promise her that. I'll be back in a bit," and then he walked onto the dance floor with Elise. She called over her shoulder to Tyson, "You can dance with someone else for a minute—why don't you ask Cassidy?"

Cassidy's eyes widened, but Tyson didn't seem the least

bit put out by Elise's request. He just held out his arm to Cassidy and said, "Shall we?"

Cassidy shot Logan a look to see if he would protest; but when he didn't, she took Tyson's arm, and they too walked to the dance floor.

For a moment neither Logan nor I said anything, and then he tilted his head at me. "I guess that leaves us. Do you want to dance?"

I held out my hand in reply. He took it in his, and we walked down to the dance floor. I was holding hands with Logan at the prom. How odd. *Surreal* was the term Mrs. Mortenson would have used. Surreal and . . . , but then I couldn't think of another word that quite fit. English 315 had failed me.

Before I could get any ideas I shouldn't have, I reminded myself that Logan didn't really want to be here with me. He wanted to be dancing with Cassidy. Just like Josh.

Logan led me to the back of the crowd and then took me loosely in his arms. I caught whiffs of his aftershave and could feel his shoulder muscles through his tux. I suddenly found it hard not to get ideas, so I glanced around the room so I didn't have to look at him.

Elise and Josh were dancing not far away. They moved across the floor, talking in a casual sort of way; and I wondered if he would pay attention to his sister, or whether any moment now his Cassidy-tracking radar would kick in and he'd ignore Elise too.

Logan put his hand on my back, and we danced slowly in rhythm to the music. I had the urge to lean in close to Logan's neck and breathe in more of his aftershave, but I didn't. Instead, I watched Josh over Logan's shoulder.

Had I been expecting too much tonight? All I had wanted

was a nice romantic evening. I'd looked forward to this night for years. I'd bought a dress, wrangled a last-minute date, decorated the room, and done my hair—all so I could have one night of romance. Instead, I was watching my date watch someone else, and I was having thoughts about a guy whose main goal for the last two weeks was to force me into going out with another guy so he could go out with another girl. It was horrible.

Logan held me a little away from him so we could talk. "So, are you having a good time tonight?"

I glanced over at Josh again. "What is it with men anyway?"

"I guess that means no."

I shook my head because I didn't want to explain. Then I shrugged and said, "I've come to the conclusion that any guy under twenty-one is terminally immature."

He winced. "Harsh. Exactly what did Josh do?"

"It's not what he did. It's just that . . ." I tilted my head up at Logan. "It's prom night—girls look forward to it. You're a guy. Tell me, why is it guys can't be romantic?"

"Ahh," Logan nodded knowingly. "I see. Josh didn't lavish you with enough compliments."

I almost said, *He hasn't paid attention to me long enough to come up with a compliment,* but instead I said, "I don't know why I asked you. You couldn't say something romantic if your life depended on it."

He grinned at me. "Sure I could."

"Prove it."

He glanced up for a moment, as though he were consulting the stars—or in this case the twinkle lights—then stared into my eyes. "You look beautiful."

"See what I mean? That isn't romantic. My mother told me the exact same thing tonight. If a mother could say it, then it doesn't count as being romantic."

"All right, I'll be more specific." Logan leaned closer to me, holding me tighter, and spoke softly into my ear. "Samantha, you look so beautiful tonight that when I came in and saw you across the room, I was glad I'd lost our bet."

I have to admit, my heart stopped beating for several seconds.

"Okay," I said slowly. "That was good, but it was probably just a fluke."

He shook his head. "What is it with girls and romance anyway?"

"If you need to ask," I said breathlessly, "you wouldn't understand."

He held me a little looser. His eyes narrowed slightly, and his brows came together. "What I want to know is this: What's wrong with being a normal sweatshirt-wearing type of guy? Girls always want some mysterious stranger who'll sweep them off their feet."

"Mysterious and stranger are optional," I said, "but sweeping is mandatory."

"You see, that's just my point. You don't want a guy with personality or substance; you just want someone who dances well and has dreamy eyes."

"You dance well." I cocked my head at him. "You have dreamy eyes too—and I could even say there are several things I find mysterious about you, like, for example, why you enjoy working on car remains. So maybe you shouldn't be so quick to categorize yourself as one of the guys with substance. . . ."

It was then I noticed Tyson and Cassidy approach Elise and Josh. Tyson cut in, taking Elise back as his partner and leaving Josh to dance with Cassidy.

Cassidy stood on the dance floor for a moment, unmoving and blushing bright pink, but Josh seemed at ease. He smiled down at her. Then he took one of her hands in his, pulled her into slow-dance position, and they began swaying back and forth.

For once Josh paid complete attention to his partner.

Logan noticed me staring and looked over to where Josh and Cassidy were dancing.

"They switched partners," I said. "I wonder if Elise and Josh planned that all along."

Logan grinned as though it didn't matter to him. "I wouldn't put it past them."

"And you don't mind?"

He shrugged. "How can I mind if Josh dances with my date? After all, I'm dancing with his."

He had a point, especially considering the fact that he'd just been whispering romantic nothings to me. Still, I stared over to where Josh stood holding Cassidy in his arms.

Logan said, "It bothers you though, doesn't it?"

I didn't say anything. I knew he was asking in a roundabout way how much I liked Josh, and I didn't know what to reply.

I pulled my gaze away from Josh and Cassidy. "It just seems so sneaky."

He lifted one eyebrow and nodded slowly. "And you've never done anything sneaky?"

"Oh, no you don't. You're not turning this dance into another one of your bash-Samantha sessions. I believe we were talking about romance and specifically your lack of it."

"I thought you said I had dreamy eyes and was mysterious."

"I was considering your potential. You weren't finished proving yourself to me."

He laughed and pulled me closer. Into my ear he said, *"Tu es très belle quand tu marches dans les vestibules, quand tu empiles des livres, et quand tu pleures."*

I didn't understand any of it—I took Spanish instead of French—but just the sound of it made me feel like my entire body could melt like a lump of candle wax onto the gym floor.

I didn't care whether Josh and Cassidy were off together. I didn't care if they ever came back. I wanted to stay here dancing with Logan, listening to French drop from his lips. Then I pushed the thought away. Logan didn't mean any of this. He was just proving a point about romance.

And a very valid point too.

Apparently I was such an idiot, my heart would race at a romantic line no matter who said it. "Very good," I said, "but knowing you, you just told me I ought to change the oil in my car every thirty thousand miles, didn't you?"

"No, I told you that you look beautiful when you walk through the hallways, when you stack books, and when you cry."

"You've never seen me cry."

"Yes, I have. In eighth grade English when we watched *Where the Red Fern Grows*. You cried at the end. That was the first time I thought you were beautiful."

"When I was crying?"

"Yeah. When you were crying."

When I cry, my face turns red and my eyes swell up. I silently considered Logan's aesthetic taste for a moment and then thought about that long-ago day in junior high. It was sweet to think of him noticing me, of him liking me back then. I let out a slow sigh. "Whatever happened to us?"

"You dumped me."

"Well, yeah, but some guys try to win girls back, you know."

"I know, but at that point you had really started to irritate me." He followed this statement with a short, "Ow!"

"I'm sorry." I smiled up at him. "Did I step on your foot? Sometimes it's hard to know where to put these pointy heels."

He limped for a couple of steps. "That is *just* the sort of thing I'm talking about."

I danced on as though nothing were different. "Don't be ridiculous. I never stepped on your foot in eighth grade. In fact, after we broke up, I was nice to you until that day in English when you decided to edit Shakespeare."

"I can't believe you still remember that."

"You took all the English books and wrote my name under *Taming of the Shrew*."

He held me away from him, as though trying to take precautions. "All right, I was mean to you first. I apologize."

"You just don't want me to step on your foot again."

Another smile crept across his face. "Well, if the pointy heels fit . . ."

I stomped my foot down, but in aggravation, not in retaliation. "Logan, you are the most frustrating—"

The music began to fade, and Logan dropped his hand from my waist. "Well, the song is over. Let's go back."

I didn't let go of his hand. "Oh no you don't. We're in the middle of a conversation. Our dates can wait for another song."

Holding tightly to his hand, I pulled him a few steps closer to the center of the dance floor. As Josh and Cassidy walked past us off the dance floor I gave them a small wave. Josh looked a bit confused, but I didn't care. It served him right if he had to stand there and watch me dance with Cassidy's date.

Logan said, "And that's another thing, Samantha, you're too bossy," but he didn't offer any other resistance. Another slow song came on, and he put his hand back on my waist and picked up the rhythm of the song.

I tilted my face up at him. "I believe you were in the middle of apologizing to me for being mean for the past three years."

"Uh, right, sorry about that."

I wanted to step on his foot again. Instead, I said, "The least you could do is tell me why you act that way."

He shrugged as though it were actually something he needed to think about. "You know in sophomore English when we put on a scene from Hamlet and you were Queen of Denmark?"

"Yeah."

"Well, a lot of times you act like you're still wearing the crown."

"I do not."

"You're running your campaign on school unity, but you're so cliquish you've spent your entire high-school existence associating only with those people who could pass for fashion models."

"I have not." Aubrie was too short to be a fashion model.

"You're only being nice to people now because you want to win the election. Afterward you'll go back to being exactly the same—a person who only thinks about herself."

Logan had said a hundred mean things to me over the years, and I had always let them roll off me. This time it hit me with a resounding thud. I could barely say anything at all for a minute, and then I wasn't sure what to say. I wanted to say, *Oh, you must want to see the beauty of me bursting into tears again,* but I couldn't pull it off in a lighthearted manner. I probably would actually burst into tears right there on the dance floor, and what was left of the evening would be ruined. My pictures would show puffy eyes and giant mascara stains, and I'd forever be known as the girl who cried at the prom.

Logan must have felt bad when I didn't say anything, because after another minute of dancing in silence, he said, "I'm sorry, Samantha. I shouldn't have said that."

Right. Of course. He wasn't at all sorry. "Go ahead and think all sorts of horrible things about me," I said. "You don't really know me at all." And then because I thought I might cry anyway, I pulled away from Logan and stormed off the dance floor. He had no choice but to follow after me, but I didn't even glance back at him.

I walked toward the table where Josh and Cassidy sat. They were looking at each other, not at me, and I heard a snatch of their conversation.

Cassidy said, "If you didn't want me to treat you coldly, then you shouldn't have broken up with me."

"I thought you could be a little more mature about this," he said.

"I'm sorry. You must have me confused with some of your other ex-girlfriends."

"Cassidy—" he said, and then noticed me walking toward him. "Samantha," he said in a startled voice, and then because he must not have known what to say, he added, "There you are."

"Yes, here I am." I forced a smile and pretended I hadn't heard them arguing. I sat down in the chair next to Josh, only slightly consoled that Cassidy and Josh weren't having a better time than Logan and I just had.

Logan came up to the table and sat down next to Cassidy but looked over at me. I put my hand possessively on Josh's arm. "Are you ready to get our pictures taken?"

"Sure." He seemed relieved. Relieved, perhaps, to get away from Cassidy?

I smiled again. I would refuse to think about Logan and all of his accusations for the rest of the night. I would only think of Josh. True, I was still a little angry at him, but thinking of him was better than thinking of Logan. And besides, now that Josh had an opportunity to get Cassidy out of his system, maybe he'd start paying attention to me. So Josh it was. He was tall, dark, and handsome, and he thought I'd grown up a lot since last year.

This thought gave me a small twinge of guilt. Josh thought I'd matured because I wasn't insulting anyone, and the only reason I wasn't insulting anyone was because of Logan's bet. Could Logan be right about the other things he'd said too?

I shook the thought off. I didn't think only of myself. I didn't.

As we walked toward the photographer I gave Josh's arm another squeeze. He smiled back at me. Which was a form of paying attention to me, which meant the evening was bound to get better. Logan was definitely so, so wrong. I wanted to turn back to him and say, *See, someone thinks I'm nice enough to date. Plus he's in college, so therefore he's smarter than you.*

Before we reached the photographer, Chelsea and Mike strolled up to us.

Chelsea gave me a hug, complimented me on the prom decorations, and then gave me a quick critique on who looked stunning, who looked so-last-season, and who looked like a hooker with a corsage. Then she turned to Josh. "Have you seen the new improvements here at PHS?"

"Improvements?" he asked.

"Vintage Samantha Taylor artwork." Chelsea took Josh's hand and pulled him toward the drinking fountain, where a couple of posters hung on the wall.

We all parked in front of one of my posters while Chelsea lifted a hand toward it in appraisement. "Notice the subtle shading and fine craftsmanship behind the lettering. One day when she's president of the United States, this will be worth money."

Josh gazed at it with placid interest. "It's really nice." What else could he say?

"It's much better than the paltry competition's," Chelsea said, pointing with a grand wave to one of Rick's posters.

It was then I looked, really looked, at the other poster. It was one of Rick's newer ones, and I hadn't seen it before. It read: RICK DEBROCK RULES THE SCHOOL. VOTE FOR RICK ON ELECTION DAY.

But that's not what caught my eye. What struck me was the *e*'s—they were tilted upward like sloppy *i*'s.

I continued to stare at the poster. In fact, for several moments that poster and my thoughts floated and twisted together, the only things existing in the universe.

Rick had made the flyers.

I knew this now, but still I couldn't fathom it. How had

he known my SAT score? Surely Cassidy wouldn't have told him. Cassidy and Rick belonged to two completely different high-school stratas. They didn't talk to each other. They had absolutely no reason to associate with each other.

Then it all fit, like puzzle pieces snapping together to finish the picture.

Chelsea had a reason, or rather Chelsea's little sister did. Chelsea said that Adrian had gone out with Rick. Suddenly, like a movie playing in my mind, I remembered exactly the time and place I told my friends about my SAT score.

I don't know what was stronger, my anger or my disappointment. I turned to Chelsea. "You told Rick my SAT score, didn't you?"

Her eyes riveted to me, and her smile vanished. "No, I didn't."

Now I was even more certain. "Yes, you did." I put my fingers across my mouth and felt my hand shaking. In a low voice I said, "I can't believe this, Chelsea—I trusted you."

She didn't say anything for a moment, and both Josh and Mike stared at us, unspeaking.

Then, as if it were almost an apology, her voice dropped. "I didn't tell *him*. I told Adrian. I didn't know she'd tell Rick about it."

"You didn't know?" My anger now outweighed my disappointment. "You just expected little Miss Black Death to keep that information to herself?"

Chelsea folded her arms, and her lips pursed into a rigid line. "Look, I didn't know Rick would make those flyers."

"You could have at least told me what you'd done, and then I wouldn't have . . ." Then I wouldn't have done an ugly thing myself by taking down Amy's posters. Then I wouldn't have blamed Cassidy for the past two weeks for betraying me.

With her arms still folded, Chelsea said, "I didn't tell you to go on a poster-tearing rampage. You guys did that all by yourselves. If I had known you were going to destroy Amy's stuff, I would have tried to stop you. But what was the point in telling you the truth after you'd already done it? I knew it would just make you feel bad."

"How noble of you." I turned and walked away from her, my dress making angry swishing sounds with every step I took back to the photographer.

I hadn't seen Josh's expression during my exchange with Chelsea, and now with him walking beside me, I was afraid to know what it was. We took our place in the back of the picture line, and for a moment neither of us said anything. Then slowly, as though he was talking to himself as much as talking to me, he said, "You tore down Amy's posters?"

And *wham*—I was no longer mature, or nice, or anything good. I was the same critical, insulting, immature girl he'd known last year. It was practically a vindication of Logan's words, and that one sentence hurt just as deeply.

I wanted to shrug the whole thing off and say, "You know how it is. All's fair in love, war, and high school." But I couldn't. I couldn't act like what I'd done didn't matter when I knew, inside, that it did.

"I made a mistake. I thought Amy wrote something horrible about me, and I retaliated."

"You weren't sure it was Amy, but you retaliated anyway?"

"I thought I was sure."

"Did you talk to her?"

Of course I didn't talk to her. She wouldn't have told me the truth— Well, actually she would have told me the truth, but I wouldn't have believed it was the truth. I couldn't tell Josh this, though. I couldn't admit to being blindly suspicious along with being vindictive. "I said it was a mistake."

"A mistake because you retaliated or a mistake because you retaliated against the wrong person?"

Either. Both. I wasn't sure, and I didn't want to think about it anymore. How much guilt should a person have to endure while waiting to get prom pictures taken? I didn't answer, but I couldn't think about anything else.

Why hadn't I just taken that flyer into the office and let them handle it?

Josh didn't press the point. We stood together in line, silently apart, until the photographer called out it was our turn. Then we went and stood side by side, hands clasped, under the archway. I smiled, but I knew the picture would turn out awful anyway. It was a fitting symbol of the evening.

After the pictures Josh and I went back to the dance floor and danced for a few more dances. The music blared out a quick tempo, and even though I tried to dance to the beat, my arms and legs suddenly felt stiff and clumsy.

Once, I noticed Logan dancing with Cassidy in a far corner. He looked perfectly happy. And why shouldn't he? He knew he'd been right about everything all along.

For the second time that night I came close to beautifying myself with tears and runny mascara. I wanted to go home; instead, I kept dancing with Josh. Every step I took, every note I heard, all seemed to echo the words in my head, "It's true . . . It's true . . ."

Finally, mercifully, the prom ended. I decided not to suggest one of the after-prom parties. Instead, when they turned up the lights, I yawned and commented on how late it was.

Josh drove me home, and we didn't talk much in the car. I knew he wanted the evening to be over as badly as I did, so it almost surprised me when he got out of the car at my house and walked me to my door—but that was the thing about Josh, he was a perfect gentleman.

He paused on the doorstep. "Thanks for asking me out, Samantha. I had a nice time."

He wasn't even a good liar; still I smiled at him anyway. "Thanks for coming. I'll give you your copy of the pictures as soon as I get them." If I didn't burn them first.

I hadn't expected him to, but he leaned forward and gave me a kiss on the cheek. "That's a friendship kiss. I want us to be friends."

"Right. Exactly." I felt like he was breaking up with me. "Well, I'll see you later."

I opened the door and went into the darkened house. Without turning on the lights, I put my purse on the hallway table and my corsage—which was now brown around the edges—into the fridge. I walked quietly up the stairs, checked in with my parents, then went to my room and kicked off my shoes. I slowly took off my earrings, necklace, and all the trappings of the evening.

The night was over, and yet in some ways it wasn't. In some ways tonight was a beginning. The person I was going to become was just beginning to form, because I couldn't stand to be the person I had been before. I could still see Josh's face looking at me with disappointment—still hear Logan's words as we danced. I went to the ball as Cinderella and then found out I was actually one of the wicked stepsisters.

I got in my pajamas and slipped into bed, trying to clear my mind of the images of the night: colorful dresses swishing around me, couples swirling by. Music blaring. I pressed my eyelids together tightly and imagined that instead of blankets, I was covered in a layer of thick green vines. Then in my mind, one by one, I turned over each leaf.

The next day I got out my extra poster board, the markers, the scrapbook stuff, and then locked myself in my room. Very carefully, I made VOTE FOR AMY posters. I couldn't undo that I'd helped tear her first ones down, but I could make her some new ones.

After dinner I went back to my room, and while I did my homework I resolved to be friendlier to everyone in school. I'd say hi to people in the hallway. I'd ask Cassidy what orphanage project she was working on next and volunteer to help. I'd even be nice to Elise. *See,* I wanted to say to Logan. *See, I'm not only thinking of myself.*

On Monday I went to school early and put the Amy posters up before anyone was around. I didn't worry too much about someone catching me; after all, there was no rule about putting posters up for an opponent.

I thought about resigning from the race. I really did. I wondered if that would be the only way to completely redeem myself for what I'd done. But then again, I hadn't actually done anything to hurt Amy's chances for winning. I hadn't smeared her name the way Rick had smeared mine. I'd just made her redo all of her posters.

These thoughts still edged around my mind as I put up the last poster. I surveyed it for a minute, then went to put the tape away in my locker. I didn't feel like standing and ogling with my friends on the front landing, so I took my biology book from my locker and sat down on the floor to read it.

I wasn't sure what to say to Chelsea or how I should act when I saw her next. I wanted to be angry and blame everything on her, but in truth I knew she hadn't set out to sabotage my campaign. Of course, she should have told me Cassidy hadn't done the sabotaging, but I even found this hard to be angry about. I kept asking myself what I would have done in Chelsea's place. If I'd made a horrible mistake and my friends had already blamed it on someone else, would I have straightened them out? Would I have done the right thing or the wrong thing?

I thought about all of the insults I'd wanted to utter over the last two weeks, Amy's posters, and the way I'd treated Cassidy.

Not only did it deflate all of my anger but it made me feel really depressed too. It seemed like the last few weeks had been nothing but a revelation of all my faults.

I flipped open my biology book and tried to push these thoughts away. The chapter heading read, "Predators and prey, the life struggle of the ecosystems." Hmm. I got to read about things killing other things. That might take my mind off my problems.

This is what I'd sunk to. I was now finding escapism in the food chain.

I hadn't read for very long before I noticed someone standing beside me. I looked up and saw Logan.

"I'm ready," he said.

"Ready for what?"

"Ready to pass out VOTE FOR SAMANTHA flyers on the front steps."

I stared at him for a moment longer, and he said, "Remember our bet?"

"Oh, yeah." I shrugged, and then returned to my book. "You don't really have to do that."

I expected him to go away, but he didn't. "Yes, I do. A bet's a bet. I would have *really* made you go out with Doug if I'd won, so now I have to *really* pass out flyers for you."

I looked back up. "You would have made me go out with Doug Campton? Doug, the *Hot Babes* calendar guy?"

When he didn't deny it, I went on with indignation. "And you accuse me of being shallow? If you had any sense of integrity, you would have died before you let me go out with Doug."

"Yeah, yeah. If I'd been trying to protect your dating schedule with my life, I would have been dead in the eighth grade."

I glared at him. It was just so easy to do.

He held out his hand to me. "So where are the flyers?"

When I didn't say anything, he said, "Really. I'll do a good job. I won't draw little mustaches on your picture or anything."

"I'm not passing them out today."

"Tomorrow then?"

I tried to find my place in my book. "I don't know."

Instead of leaving, he sat down by me. He leaned over and said, "Would this have anything to do with the fact that you made posters for Amy?"

I still stared down at my book. "Who said I made posters for Amy?"

He sighed, then took the book from my hands. I grabbed for it, but he held it to his side, away from me. I would have had to crawl over him to get it, and I wasn't about to do that. I looked at his face to see why he was being so difficult, and when I did, he said, "I've only known you for forever, Samantha. I recognize your handwriting. I see it on every book order you place."

"Oh." I hadn't counted on this possibility. I wondered who else would recognize my handwriting and if I would be answering this question all day. What would I say to all the people who asked me why I'd made posters for my competitor?

"Well?" he asked. He wasn't waiting around for me to come up with a well-thought-out explanation.

"I did it because . . ."

"Because you were the one who tore down Amy's posters?"

"Who told you that?" Was it common knowledge? Had everyone known all along that I'd done it? The thought made my heart pound in my chest. Everyone thought less of me.

Logan smiled like it was a silly question. "I figured it was either you or Rick, and it's your handwriting on the new Amy posters."

"Oh." I blushed at being so easily caught. Slowly I said, "It was in retaliation for making those flyers about me. Only I just found out it was Rick who actually made the flyers, so I . . ."

"Made new posters for Amy."

"Don't tell anyone."

"I won't." He handed my book back to me and said softly, "For what it's worth, you have my vote."

He smiled at me then, and it's funny, but that smile meant

more to me than anything had for a long time. He stood up to go, but before he walked off, he said, "We're still on for dinner on Saturday, right? You're not letting me off on that part of the bet are you?"

"Naw," I said back. "I still have a craving for lobster."

After fourth period, instead of walking to the cafeteria like I usually did, I walked over to Cassidy's locker. She was just pulling her lunch bag out.

"Hi," I said, "do you have a minute?"

She shut her locker door. "Sure," but she said the word tightly, as though she wasn't pleased about talking to me for even sixty seconds.

I gripped my own lunch sack tighter. "Cassidy, I owe you an apology. I just wanted to let you know I'm sorry about everything. I was wrong."

She stared at me with surprise. "About Josh?"

"Well, I was talking about those flyers; but sure, now that you mention it, I was wrong about Josh too."

"What do you mean you were wrong about Josh?" Her voice was edged with anger, like she thought I might be insulting him.

"I just mean it was wrong of me to go out with him when he was so clearly interested in you." A mistake I wouldn't repeat if for no other reason than my ego couldn't take more of that type of abuse.

"Oh." Relief softened her face, but a moment later it was gone. "He's only interested in me now because there's no one else around."

"Thanks. I was around."

"I didn't mean it that way. I just meant that, well . . ." She took a deep breath, and I could tell she wasn't sure whether she should say more—that she wasn't sure whether or not she could trust me with her feelings on the matter—but then, perhaps because I'd just apologized to her, she said, "When Josh was at college surrounded by other girls, he didn't want a long-distance relationship with me. That wasn't good enough for him. But now, now that he's home for the summer, he's being nice to me."

"You don't want to be second-best. I know the feeling." And suddenly it seemed almost funny that Cassidy and I had something in common. We could have formed the Rejected by Josh Club. Only I suppose since neither of us wanted to be second-best, we would have had a hard time deciding who should be vice president.

Cassidy nodded. "It's like he just wants a summer girlfriend. Once school starts again, it will be all over, all over again."

Part of me wanted to nod in agreement and say, "Yeah, men are horrible creatures, and Josh is especially horrible because he never liked me," but another part of me, the better part, felt obligated to say something else.

"If he just wanted a summer girlfriend, he could have chosen anyone, and I can testify that he's not the least bit interested in me. I think he's being nice to you because he likes you."

She smiled, but then forced it away. "Well, maybe it's not his choice this time. Maybe I don't want to be his girlfriend again."

"Uh-huh. He's gorgeous, premed, and can't take his eyes off you when you're in the room."

"Really?"

"I'd tell you all about the prom, but I'm trying to repress that memory."

"He couldn't take his eyes off me?"

I laughed. It felt nice to talk to her. It felt easy. As we turned to walk to the cafeteria I said, "I give you approximately one week till you're back together."

"Definitely not. My pride can hold up at least two weeks." She bit her lip. "Well, maybe a week and a half."

My friends were already eating their lunches when I arrived. They all looked at me with uncertainty as I sat down, so I knew Chelsea had told them what happened between the two of us at the prom.

"There you are," Rachel said. "We were wondering if you were at school today."

"I had some biology stuff to do this morning, and I was late to lunch because I went to talk to Cassidy, you know, trying to make amends."

Aubrie leaned in closer and shot me a wide-eyed look of sympathy. "What did you say?"

"Basically that I'd been wrong, and I was sorry."

Chelsea winced, and then put her hand near mine on the table. "Really, Samantha, I'm so sorry you had to go through that. It must have been awful."

"Not in the way you think. She was very nice about it."

"I bet she really laid a guilt trip on you, didn't she?" Rachel said.

"No, she was nice about it."

"Like right," Chelsea said. "Just wait and see what happens the next time she's out campaigning for Amy."

Rachel nodded in agreement. "She puts on such an act of being sweet. You'd think her main goal in life was to be sprinkled on the top of breakfast cereal."

"She was very nice about it," I said again, this time more firmly.

"Why do you keep saying that?" Chelsea asked.

"She's still on her no-insult kick," Aubrie said.

Rachel looked over at me. "Wasn't that supposed to be over on Friday?"

I shrugged as I took my sandwich out of its bag. "Maybe I'm just tired of being so critical. Maybe we all could stand to be a little nicer."

Chelsea opened her mouth as though about to protest, but then didn't. She probably still felt so guilty about the flyers she would have supported me even if I'd just suggested that we all take up clogging.

Rachel leaned back in her chair and took a bag of chips from her lunch sack. "Oh, come on."

But Aubrie nodded. "I don't suppose it would hurt if we were less critical."

Rachel humphed. "I'm not that critical to begin with."

"Think you could go two weeks without criticizing someone?" I asked.

"Probably," she said.

Chelsea shook her head, then picked up her fork. "I think Doug is going to get a date out of this one way or the other."

"Yeah," Aubrie said, "but it might be with you."

And then we all laughed, at least we all laughed except for Rachel, who went on to vigorously protest that she wasn't the critical type.

On Tuesday three things of importance happened—the first one being that when I came to school I ran into Logan passing out flyers in the front lobby. When I got close to him, he winked at me, then handed a flyer to a passing student and in a loud voice said, “Vote for Samantha, she’s really not all that bad.”

“Very funny.” I took a flyer to see what it said. It had my name down one side, and in the middle of the paper it said, VOTE FOR SAMANTHA. SHE’S TAYLOR-MADE FOR THE PRESIDENCY. A little candy bar was taped on the bottom of each flyer.

“Catchy,” I said. “Where did you get them?”

“Chelsea made them. She’s passing out more of them upstairs.”

“How nice.” I knew it was her way of apologizing, and despite the last couple of days, I knew everything would be all right between us.

The second thing was that I talked to Amy. I hadn’t said much to her, well, ever, but I had said even less to her since the campaign started. Now I sought her out. I walked around the hallway by her locker until she finally showed up. While she pulled color-coded folders from her locker I went and stood beside her. "Look, I'm not really good at apologies; but I thought you made that flyer about me, so I tore down your first set of posters. I'm sorry I did it, and if you turn me in—well, I'll understand."

She stopped shuffling her folders for a moment. "Oh."

I wasn't sure what that meant, and I shifted my weight uncomfortably while I waited for her to say something else.

Finally she said, "I wouldn't feel right about getting you in trouble. I mean, if I win this election, I want it to be because the students like my ideas and want me as their president. Not because the only other choice was some guy whose platform consisted of beer and anarchy."

"Thanks." And then because I really respected her at that moment, I added, "And if I win, I'd like your help running things. I think you're really smart and organized."

She smiled. "Thanks. And if I win, I'd like your help too. I think you're really . . . um . . . popular."

Sometimes it's just better not to compliment people. Still, I smiled and said, "I'm glad there are no hard feelings."

And there weren't. I mean, I couldn't hold it against Amy that she couldn't think of any presidential skills I had. After all, the only thing she'd ever seen me do was lead cheers. Once this was all over, though, I was going to make an effort to get to know her better.

The third thing that happened was that I met up alone with Rick.

Ever since I noticed the poster at the prom, I'd thought off and on what I'd say to him the next time I had a chance. Part of me wanted to scream at him. I wanted to take him by his shoulders and shake all his safety pins loose. I wanted to tell him he and his stupid flyers were the root of all my problems, and everything bad that had happened to me over the last couple weeks was his fault.

But that wasn't entirely true. And besides, he'd enjoy knowing all the trauma he'd caused me.

I seriously thought about not saying anything at all and just taking a marker to his posters. I wanted to go up to every single RICK ROCKS poster and pen the word EATS in the middle.

I couldn't do it, though. Destroying posters was what got me into trouble in the first place. I didn't want to do it again.

I really wished I could take the high ground on the matter. I wanted to walk up to Rick with an aloof stare and say, "I would never stoop to your level."

But I already had. I wished so badly I could go back in time, back to before I ripped down Amy's posters, so I could stop myself. Then I'd feel justified marching Rick and his flyer into the office and nailing both of them to the principal's desk. But how could I do that when I hadn't used good campaigning tactics, either?

So I didn't say anything to the principal, and I didn't know what to say to Rick. And then during fifth period while I ran an errand for my biology teacher, I nearly tripped over Rick on the stairs. He sat sprawled on the landing, head tilted back, eyes half open, listening to a Walkman.

He was probably cutting class. It figured. I was doing everything I could to try and get into a good college, and Rick was skipping school. Had he ever, for even one moment, thought of his future?

And what would his future be?

As soon as this thought occurred to me, I felt sorry for him, and it was probably that one instant of sympathy that kept me from kicking him as I walked by. Instead, I stood in front of him, hands on my hips, and waited for him to notice me.

He pushed one of the headphones off of his ear. "Yeah?"

I still didn't know what to say to him. I stood there simultaneously reliving picking up those flyers from the parking lot and remembering every lesson on forgiveness I'd ever had.

I didn't move. "Hey."

A snarl grew on his face, and he pushed the OFF button on his Walkman. "You want something, Taylor?"

His snarl brought my anger back. "Yeah, I do." I wanted him to tell me he was sorry. I wanted him to borrow a conscience for two minutes, just so he could understand what he'd done. I also wanted to be able to think of the perfect thing to say to him to show him how I felt.

But that was impossible. *I* wasn't even sure how I felt. And with so many emotions running through me, I was afraid if I said anything, I'd say everything and never stop.

I'd spit out: *Speaking of Rick's rocks, which one did you just crawl out from underneath?*

And if you're going to stick sharp objects through your head, do us all a favor and aim for a lobotomy next time.

And I notice you didn't report your *test scores anywhere on that flyer. I suppose there's a good reason for that.*

But as I stood there I kept thinking, *What is his future going to be?* And I couldn't say any of those things to him. I didn't want to. I was completely and horribly reformed.

I dropped my hands from my hips and shrugged. "I just

want to tell you good luck on your campaign." Then I smirked. I couldn't help myself. "And may the best candidate win."

Which, of course, excluded Rick.

Okay, maybe I wasn't *completely* reformed.

I turned and walked away from him, still smirking when I reached the bottom of the stairs.

For the next three days I spent all of my free time either campaigning or worrying about the election. Sometimes I imagined how it would feel when the principal looked me in the eye and said, "Congratulations, Samantha, you're our new president." Other times I worried that if it were Amy's or Rick's eyes the principal looked into, I'd do something to humiliate myself—like scream, or cry, or perhaps be struck dumb for several moments.

I also spent a lot of time doodling the initials LH in my notebook, but then I crossed them out before anyone could see them. I was almost afraid to think of how our date on Saturday would go. Logan would probably be obnoxious the whole time, or beg me for another chance with Veronica, or do something equally terrible. Then I'd have to throw my lobster at him, and the whole night would be ruined.

Was it too much to ask for just one nice evening with Logan?

On Friday morning before the vote, everyone assembled in the gym, and we gave our election speeches. You would have thought that after years of jumping around in a short skirt in front of the entire school that nothing would frighten me, but as I stood to give my talk I felt as though my knees had deserted me.

I'd actually written four different speeches and decided I didn't like any of them. I finally chose a short and direct one. I told the student body I knew I could do the job, and if elected, I would do my best to represent them. It didn't have the hype I'd put in the earlier four versions, but somehow I just couldn't do hype. I couldn't promote myself on hoopla. If people voted for me, I wanted it to be because they believed in me.

Rick gave a talk that was half stand-up comedy and half social commentary. He received a lot of hoots throughout.

Amy gave a rundown of every program the student body was in charge of and how she'd improve each one. She brought in charts to illustrate her points. Everyone clapped politely for her, as they had for all of us, and when the speeches were over, I still wasn't sure which of us had the lead.

The principal spoke to us for a few minutes about the blessings and responsibilities of living in a democratic society and then dismissed us to our classes so we could vote. During fifth period all the candidates were called down to the front office so they could tell us the election results before they announced them on the PA system.

When I walked in the front office, I noticed Rick, Amy, and most of the other candidates standing around in front of the attendance desk, fidgeting and looking as uncomfortable as I felt. A few people talked quietly to one another; but most of us just stared around the room, fingering our books while we waited for the remaining people to show up. When they did, the principal escorted us to her office.

We listened silently as she talked about how we should all be proud of ourselves for the job we'd done, and so on and so on. Then she unfolded a piece of paper and read the results. First she told us who the new secretary, treasurer, and vice president were. Then without even pausing, she said, "And the president will be Amy Stock."

On the positive side, I didn't cry or scream, or even become mute. I felt myself turn, almost automatically, to Amy and say, "Congratulations. I know you'll do a great job."

"Yeah, congratulations," Rick mumbled.

Amy looked back and forth between us, and then to the principal. "I can't believe I won. I just can't believe it."

That made three of us.

It wasn't that I didn't want to be happy for her, I was just too busy being devastated for me to muster much enthusiasm. I wanted to go home and lock myself in my room for a long time.

"You all did a fine job with your speeches and your campaigns," the principal told us. "I hope you learned something valuable from the process and will try again sometime."

Oh, yeah. I'd just spent four weeks of my life trying to convince people to like me, all so I could come into this office and have my hopes and dreams shattered. I was not exactly eager to repeat the process, but I smiled at the principal anyway. "Thanks. Maybe I will."

It was all I could do to make it through the rest of what was left of the school day. I mean, how many times should a person have to say, "It's okay. I know Amy will be a great president," when I really wanted to say, "Did you vote for her and not me?"

I suppose it's a good thing I didn't know who came in second place. It would have killed me to know I lost to Rick too. At least this way I could imagine it had been very close between Amy and me and that only three people voted for Rick.

After school Chelsea, Aubrie, and Rachel offered to drive me to Baskin Robbins so I could drown my sorrow in double fudge brownie, but I took a rain check. I just wanted to go home, where I could fall apart in private; and although I didn't come right out and tell them so, they seemed to understand.

On the way driving home, I decided to tell my mother about my SAT score. No matter how upset she got, I couldn't feel more awful than I already did, so it was good timing. Ranting, raving, threatening—none of these things would even faze me. Besides, now that my political hopes had been squelched, Mom needed to get used to the idea that I wasn't going to college. I was going to be one of those people who lived on a street corner, mumbled things no one understood, and ate discarded Big Macs. In my spare time I'd try to catch pigeons. It would be an easy, carefree life.

Mom was unpacking groceries into the refrigerator when I walked into the kitchen. I got a glass from the cupboard, then went to the sink to get some water. I took a long drink, a deep breath, and blurted out, "I lost the election, I bombed my SAT test, and I've given up any hope of having a happy future."

Mom shut the refrigerator door. "You lost the election? Oh honey, I'm sorry—" Then she stopped, and I could almost see her processing the rest of the information. "What did you say about the SAT?"

"I bombed it."

"What do you mean, you bombed it?"

"I got a three hundred and fifty on the math portion. It dragged my score down." I didn't mention that my other score didn't have very far to drag.

Mom shut her eyes and opened them slowly. She was on the verge of a lecture—you could almost see the words "What have you been doing all these years during your math classes?" about to spring from her lips. But she didn't say them. Instead, she asked, "What was your composite?"

"Eight hundred and ten."

"Eight hundred and ten?" Mom looked up at the ceiling, then back at me with a cold stare. "When did you find out about your score?"

"A few weeks ago."

Mom took a box of cereal from the grocery bag, shoved it into the cupboard, and slammed the cupboard door shut. "So basically, everyone but your parents knew your score all along, and you didn't tell us so I could make a fool of myself in front of everyone by insisting you hadn't got your scores yet." She then took a loaf of bread and flung it into the bread box with enough force to ensure we'd be eating three-inch sandwiches all week. "I even called the school and complained that your scores hadn't come in."

Quietly I said, "I didn't tell you because I didn't want you to be angry."

"Well, that worked out really well. I'm not angry at all now."

Tears stung my eyes, and I didn't try to stop them from

coming. "This isn't about you. It's my score, my problem, and I feel really awful about it. It would be nice if you could just be a little sad for me."

I didn't wait for her to answer. I turned and walked out of the kitchen and upstairs to my bedroom. Once there, I lay down on my bed and buried my face in my pillow to muffle the sound of my crying.

After a few minutes Mom walked into the room. I didn't even know she'd come in until she sat down on my bed. She put her hand on my back and said, "I'm sorry, Samantha. I handled that all wrong. I shouldn't have yelled." She rubbed her hand slowly across my back. "I make a lot of mistakes as a parent, but I'm trying to be better. Isn't that as much as any of us can do?"

I sat up and gave her a hug, and she held me for a while. I know she never thought I listened to her, but her words kept repeating in my mind. "I'm trying to be better. Isn't that as much as any of us can do?"

I wanted so badly for those words to be true for me too. "I'm sorry about everything," I said.

"Things will seem better tomorrow. We'll talk about what we can do to help your studies."

I nodded, even though I had the feeling what-we-could-do would probably involve things that were hard, painful, and required me to sit in front of textbooks for long hours.

Still, I felt better about my score when she left. I wondered why I didn't tell her in the very beginning about it, instead of carrying the secret around like a lead weight.

I lay there for a while longer, staring at the ruffle on my pillow sham while I tried to figure out how much my GPA would rise if I aced all of my finals.

A few moments later Mom opened my door and peered in at me. "Logan Hansen is here to see you."

"Why?"

Mom shrugged. "The guys who come to see you generally don't give me lengthy explanations when I let them in. Why don't you go downstairs and ask him."

If it had been anyone else in the world, I would have told my mother to send him away. Santa Claus himself could have shown up to explain his whereabouts since my childhood, and I would have turned him out.

But somehow I wanted to see Logan, or at least I wanted to know why he'd come by. Before I left, I checked my reflection in the mirror. My eyes were puffy, but there was nothing I could do about that. I trudged down the stairs. Logan was waiting for me by the front door.

"I suppose you think I look beautiful," I said.

"I do." He nodded toward the coat closet. "Get your jacket. If we catch an early dinner, we'll have time for a movie."

"I thought we weren't going out till Saturday."

He shrugged. "You need someone to cheer you up today."

My eyes were swollen, and I didn't want to pretend I was in an upbeat mood. "Thanks, Logan, but I don't think tonight will work out."

"Why not?"

I said the only thing I could think of. "I've got homework to do."

He folded his arms across his chest. "*Now* you want to get serious about your schoolwork? Now, when I'm trying to take you out?"

I smiled despite myself. Somehow Logan made me feel as

though things could be normal again. Suddenly I did want to go out with him, but still I hesitated.

"Go on," he said. "Get your jacket, purse, and all that girl stuff you women lug around on dates. I've got reservations at the Hilltop, and they won't hold the window seats forever."

I found myself walking up the stairs to get my things, even though I still hadn't quite decided to go with him.

"Bring your homework along too," he called after me. "We'll work on it while we wait for dinner."

"And to think I accused you of not knowing how to be romantic," I called back. I went to my room and picked up my jacket and purse but left my homework on my desk.

When I came back downstairs, he was leaning against the doorway. "I know how to be romantic. I thought I'd already proven that to you."

"Oh yeah, at the prom, when you told me I was cliquish."

"If you recall, I said other things too."

"Some of which made me step on your foot."

He nodded thoughtfully. "I remember that. You'd better not wear heels tonight."

I called to my mom that I was going to dinner with Logan, and she yelled back, "Don't stay out too late."

Then Logan opened the front door for me, and we walked to his car. I got in silently, and so did he. Perhaps neither of us felt like small talk. I stared out the window as he pulled into the street and wondered if we'd drive all the way to the restaurant without speaking. Finally he said, "You know, Samantha, being president would have been nice, but you have a lot of other opportunities to do things with our class next year. And if you want to go into politics, you'll have other chances. Just remember, Abraham Lincoln lost half a dozen elections before he won the presidency."

I wondered, but I didn't ask, what Lincoln's SAT scores had been.

Instead, I fiddled with the safety belt strap on my lap and decided I'd better tell Logan the truth about my political ambitions, or I'd have to endure an entire evening of presidential triumph stories.

I looked at the safety belt latch and not at Logan. "It's nice of you to try and cheer me up, but I just ran for president so I'd have a better chance of getting into a good college. I have no idea how I'm going to be accepted anywhere decent now."

He looked over at me for a moment, then turned his attention back to the road. "That's it? That's the only reason you wanted to be president? I stood on the steps and told people to vote for you all because you wanted something impressive to put on your college application?"

He had a way of always making everything seem so bad.

"It was your idea," I said. "You were the one who told me they look at your leadership qualifications."

He shook his head and let out a sigh. I thought he'd break into some sort of lecture, but instead he said, "Well, you can always put down that you're head cheerleader."

"They'd count that?"

"They count a lot of stuff. Of course, you're still going to have to study to pull up your grades and get a decent SAT score."

"But what if it still isn't enough?"

"Well, then you go where you can get admitted and get good grades so you can transfer to the school you want to go to."

It wouldn't have been my choice of answers. I would have preferred Logan to offer up a magic solution, something quick, easy, and painless; but I knew it couldn't be that way. This was one of those things only hard work would solve.

"Your friends can help you study," he said.

"Yeah. My friends are such study-holics."

"Not your cheerleading friends. I'm talking about your other friends. Me, for example."

He was my friend? Good news. "All right. When do you like to study?"

He pulled into the Hilltop parking lot, and in a completely serious voice said, "Mostly on Friday nights."

"Friday nights?"

"I know it's your big date night, but you'll just have to tell the Brads and Joshes of the world that you have more important things to do."

He got out of the car, then went around and opened the door for me with a flourish. He waved a hand toward the restaurant and with a French accent said, "Mademoiselle, your lobster awaits." Then as I climbed out he gave me a killer smile.

I looked over at him suspiciously. "Why are you being so nice to me? Last weekend you told me you didn't even like me."

He shut the car door, but didn't walk toward the restaurant. "I never said I didn't like you."

"You said I was insulting, annoying, and thought only about myself."

"But I never said I didn't like you."

I tilted my head at him and crossed my arms. "It's the same thing."

"No, it's not, because even when you were insulting, annoying, and thought only about yourself, I still couldn't help but like you. That was one of the reasons you were so annoying."

"Romance, and now flattery too. How did I ever let you go the first time?" I started to walk toward the restaurant, but he reached out, took my hand, and pulled me back to where he stood. His voice was suddenly serious. "You've changed, Samantha, and so have I. I think it's a good change, don't you?"

I didn't know exactly what he was referring to, and yet I knew exactly what he meant. "Yes," I said.

Then he leaned over, right there in the restaurant parking lot, and kissed me. And it wasn't a friendship kiss, either. It was tender and real, and utterly romantic.

After a moment Logan seemed to remember we were in a parking lot, and he let me go but kept hold of my hand.

My heart was still pounding against my chest, and I didn't know what to say next. Finally I smiled up at him. "Do you still want me to go out with Doug?"

He smiled back at me. "I'd rather die first."

I laughed, and suddenly I felt like everything had worked out exactly as it was supposed to. Logan squeezed my hand and said, "Poor Doug."

"Poor Veronica," I agreed, and squeezed his hand back.